PARADISE ON FIRE

Jewell Parker Rhodes

Illustrations by
Serena Malyon

(L)(B)

LITTLE, BROWN AND COMPANY
New York   Boston

Little, Brown and Company
Hachette Book Group
1290 Avenue of the Americas, New York, NY 10104
Visit us at LBYR.com

First Edition: September 2021

Little, Brown and Company is a division of Hachette Book Group, Inc. The Little, Brown name and logo are trademarks of Hachette Book Group, Inc.

The publisher is not responsible for websites (or their content) that are not owned by the publisher.

Library of Congress Cataloging-in-Publication Data
Names: Rhodes, Jewell Parker, author.
Title: Paradise on fire / Jewell Parker Rhodes.
Description: First edition. | New York : Little, Brown and Company, 2021. | Includes bibliographical references. | Audience: Ages 8–12. | Summary: Bronx middle-grader Addy, who struggles with a family tragedy by drawing maps and studying mazes, joins other city youngsters on a wilderness adventure in California that turns deadly when wildfires erupt.
Identifiers: LCCN 2021001033 | ISBN 9780316493833 (hardcover) | ISBN 9780316282123 (ebook other) | ISBN 9780316493840 (ebook)
Subjects: CYAC: Wilderness areas—Fiction. | Wildfires—Fiction. | Survival—Fiction. | Grief—Fiction. | Orphans—Fiction. | African Americans—Fiction.
Classification: LCC PZ7.R3476235 Par 2021 | DDC [Fic]—dc23
LC record available at https://lccn.loc.gov/2021001033

ISBNs: 978-0-316-49383-3 (hardcover),
978-0-316-49384-0 (ebook)

Printed in the United States of America

LSC-C

Printing 1, 2021

To Wildfire Survivors

Past, Present, and Future

Forever Mourning Those Lost

FLYING BLIND

I

"There's always a way out," Grandma Bibi whispers. "Use your mind, your heart." Her arthritic fingers poke my chest.

Closing my eyes, I smell her red bush tea, the shea butter she rubs on her skin. Her spirit is alive, urgent.

But Grandma Bibi isn't here.

Here is a packed airplane. The plane is leveling off, engines murmuring steadily. Two bells. The seat belt sign blinks off. We're flying high.

I grab my pencil and notepad from my backpack and draw. I remember the flight attendant, walking the aisle, pointing at emergency exit doors.

I quickly sketch row after row. (I block the front exit with an **X**.) The closest exits are ahead of me. Row 18. Exits on the left and right. These are my escape doors.

If the plane falls, drops through the sky, I need to rush from row 23 to row 18. I'm in the window seat. I need to get past the two kids sitting on my right. Should I go forward or back? If the aisle is packed, then what? Retreat to my seat? Cling, swing, window shade to window shade to safety? Climb over seats? What's the best path?

I underline **ESCAPE** three times.

"What's that?"

I roll my eyes. Press my pencil, snapping the lead. My new line is blurred, crooked. Blocking the path.

"I'm Jay," says the boy next to me. "Jay from Brooklyn."

Jay has a high-top fade with precision cuts on the sides. His brows bushy, his eyes brown, he's the cocky know-it-all type.

He doesn't know me. I keep drawing, mapping

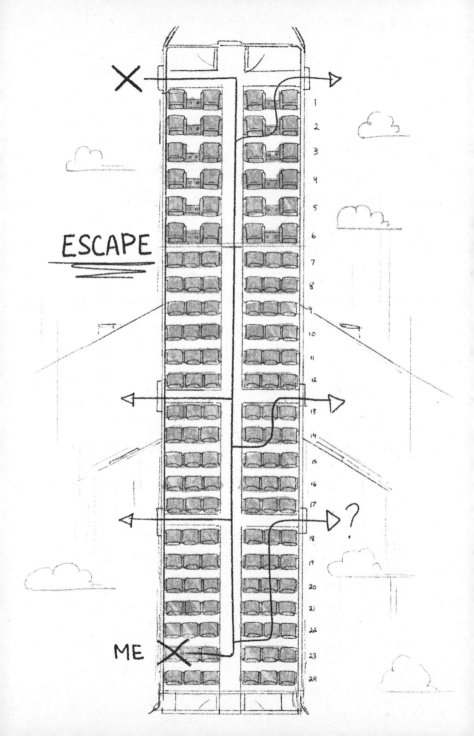

space, mirroring row upon row. Sketching arrows, leading to possible paths out.

"It's a maze, isn't it?" asks the girl in the aisle seat. "Where you have to figure a way in? Or out."

"Nope." I flip a page and quickly sketch. "*This* is a maze."

ESCAPE is in the center. Around it, like it's a magical, hidden door, I twist and turn the seats, creating false starts, incomplete paths.

Even though Jay and the girl are watching me, I can tell I'm confusing them.

Broken lines. Dead ends. Incomplete openings. That's what a maze does. Disrupts progress, confuses direction. Complicates.

"Hey, I used to have a book of mazes." The girl reaches past Jay, takes my pencil, and tries to solve the puzzle.

"Wrong way," Jay says excitedly. "Go left."

She hits a dead end. Again and again.

"Let me try."

Jay's blocked, too.

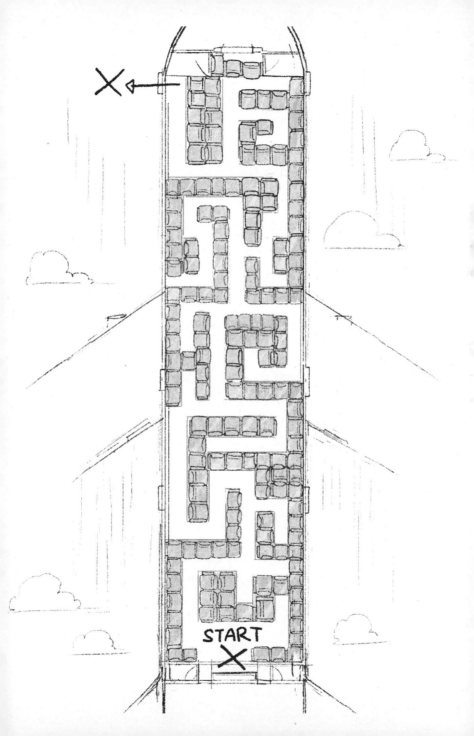

START

The girl grabs the pencil, focusing, drawing the line in fits and starts.

She's trying hard. Intense eyes. Black braids. Her teeth scratch at her bottom lip.

"Show us," she pleads.

Like always, I solve the puzzle first in my mind. Then I move the pencil forward, zigzagging, no back turns, until I reach EXIT.

"Wow. You're good."

"How'd you do that?" asks Jay, surprised.

"There's a trick to it." It's easier to solve a maze from EXIT back to START.

(Besides, when you make the maze, you always win. You control the view.)

The girl extends her hand in front of and across Jay's belly.

"Jersey City," she says. "I'm from Jersey. Nessa for Vanessa."

I blink, saying nothing. I'm not used to kids reaching out to be friends with me.

I shake Nessa's hand. Jay's, too.

* * *

We're sitting in the back, behind the plane's wings. Seats A, B, C, D, E, F—all filled with Black kids. We're supposed to bond. Be friends.

I want to return to the Bronx. To Bibi. But she made me go.

"To know yourself, you need to journey, Adaugo. Remember what's forgotten."

I love Grandma Bibi. Whatever she wants, I try to do.

"That's Kelvin, A'Leia, and DeShon." Nessa, the "social one," points across the aisle.

Kelvin and A'Leia wave.

"They're from Philly."

DeShon, eyes closed, not taking off his headphones, bobs his head, slapping his thigh to a beat.

Nessa frowns. "He doesn't talk much."

"You talk enough for everyone," Jay teases.

Nessa sticks out her tongue.

Kelvin and A'Leia wear glasses. A'Leia's are

thick with black trim; Kelvin's glasses are thin purple squares. A'Leia wears an oversized varsity jacket. Basketball, I think. Jay wears orange track shoes and a T-shirt: JUST DO IT. Nessa wears color-coordinated pink leggings and a skirt. Kelvin and DeShon wear black T-shirts and jeans.

Ordinary kids—smiling, chatting, laughing. They're not alert, scanning the plane, watching close when people clog the aisle. They're different than me. Relaxed. They fit in.

Maybe Kelvin, A'Leia, Jay, Nessa, and DeShon wanted to go to California? Universal Studios, beaches, movie stars. Los Angeles Lakers.

Maybe they were forced?

Nope. Get real.

They probably thought, *Ooooo, a plane ride. An adventure.* And it's FREE.

What's not to like?

No hot, city boredom. No same old, same old.

Still, I like sitting on the apartment's front steps, watching kids play pickup, double Dutch. I even like listening to the girls gossiping about who's cute, who's not. Even though they don't include me, they don't mind me knowing who has a crush on Jermaine. They don't mind braiding hair, painting nails, while I sit one step behind them, drawing maps, studying mazes. They notice I'm different. Being an orphan is like being a crusted-over scab. Leave me alone. Don't touch.

I stare out the window. Pancake clouds float. Mountain clouds burst, scatter as the plane flies through them. Seeing the open air unnerves me, reminds me of something—what?

My heart races. I slam the shade down.

I look at my escape map, then lean forward, lifting from the seat pocket the laminated safety card. "Did you study this?"

Jay shrugs, acting cool. "Nothing's going to happen."

Like me, I think this is Jay's first time flying. Probably like all of us.

"If something happens, I'll follow you," says Nessa, giggling. "What's your name?"

I don't want to say. Saying my name means I'm really here. Means this trip is real. I'm long gone. Far from home. Flying cross-country to Los Angeles. Six hours, 1,543 miles.

"Fate. No deny, Adaugo." The memory of Bibi's voice rattles me. *"Daughter of an eagle. You must go."*

I swallow. Funny, I draw maps but I don't travel.

Nessa watches me. Not mean, just curious.

"Addy," I say. "My name is Addy."

Jay's brows lift.

Nessa exclaims, "Pretty. Nice name."

In front of us, camp counselor Jamie, a blond girl, stands, turns. "Are we having fun yet?"

Across the aisle, lanky, curly-haired Dylan, his finger stabbing the air, talks down at Kelvin, A'Leia, and DeShon. DeShon ignores him. Kelvin and A'Leia, intent, listen closely.

Jamie and Dylan are college students, camp counselors teaching in a summer program: Wilderness Adventures.

We're a special charity. Black city kids going west. Jamie and Dylan are going to show us how to live. How to be cowboys. Cowgirls.

I wonder: How come I can't show them how I live in New York, the Bronx?

Jamie has a happy smile. It bugs me. Happy people always bug me.

"If the plane starts falling, you going to lead us out?" I demand.

Jamie's smile slides off her face. "The plane isn't going to fall."

"But if it does. Are you responsible for us?"

Jamie blinks like she doesn't understand.

"In an emergency. Are you responsible for us in an emergency? Like a teacher?"

Me, Jay, and Nessa—we all stare.

Jamie, red-faced, answers, "Of course I am." Then she twists, slumps in her seat.

I'm disgusted. I stare at my map. Many pathways. But only one path that's best for escape.

Jay leans, whispers in my ear, "Not sure anyone survives a plane crash."

I don't look at him. "I will."

Then I roll my sweater into a makeshift pillow and close my eyes. I don't open them when the attendant asks, "Drinks? Water? Coke?"

I breathe evenly, pretending sleep as Jay and Nessa munch on peanuts, pretzels. Jay shifts and I squint, watching him lift the safety guide from the seat. He studies it, his head bent, his finger drawing a path like I drew lines on my maze.

Maybe Jay isn't so bad after all?

I sigh and widen my eyes a bit, seeing Nessa slyly studying me. She's smart, too, I think.

I go back to pretending sleep.

I remember Bibi, at the airport, hugging me, murmuring, *"You're always journeying whether you like it or not."*

I try to relax. My hands rest on my pocket where my map is tucked inside.

No matter what: Escape. Survive.

II

"Why couldn't we stay in LA? It's boring driving these freeways."

"What part of *wilderness adventure* don't you understand?" Jay exclaims, scowling at Kelvin.

DeShon is still listening to his music, his head nodding, jerking. A'Leia is trying to text. The signal keeps getting lost.

It's hard to stay awake in the too-warm van. Jamie, Dylan, and the driver are in the front row, soaking up the air-conditioning. Us kids are roasting in the back.

Nessa, twirling a braid, stares out the window at the speeding cars. Fourteen-lane highways. "Unbelievable," she mutters. "They need subways."

"Monorails like Disneyland," insists Kelvin.

"Or an **L**, elevated trains like in Chicago," Jay tells a skeptical Kelvin. "I've seen photos."

"I've never been to Chicago," responds Kelvin. "Never been anywhere but Philly and here."

"Me either," says Nessa. "Except it's New Jersey and here."

I don't add "Me either," though it's true. Though "here" isn't anywhere yet...just a map of packed concrete highways crisscrossing overhead, curving, making figure eights. Snake twists. The patterns are amazing.

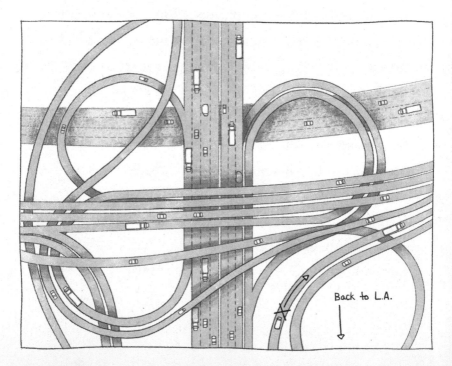

Back to L.A.

Many roads to get in, get out. Our van chooses the right ramp. I'm keeping track of where we've been. Arrow back to LA. The airport. Fly home.

"Say goodbye to civilization," says Dylan, pointing right. The van slows.

Outside the window, it's like an old-time postcard. Maybe thirty single-story homes, mostly painted white, and mobile homes (which I've never seen before!). There're a couple of roads. Some flower gardens. Chickens. A couple of horses.

A boy—maybe eight?—runs toward the road. He's waving, a big smile on his face. A'Leia and Nessa "Oooo" and wave back.

The van pulls farther away. I twist in my seat, looking out the back window. The boy still stands by the side of the road, arms dangling. Distance makes him disappear.

"Any Black people live in that town?" asks Kelvin.

A'Leia pokes him.

"Ow, I'm just trying to figure out how different this place is from home."

"We're not in Kansas anymore," I say.

"Kansas?" Kelvin squints behind his glasses. "What's that mean?"

"Nothing," adds Jay. "Just another place we've never been."

"What does it matter?" asks Nessa, exasperated.

I'm not sure what Nessa means—it doesn't matter if the town is all white? Or that we haven't been anywhere?

"Dorothy lives in Kansas," A'Leia murmurs. "*Wizard of Oz.*"

For hours, we drive. No one says anything. The air conditioner blows. The engine hums, sometimes whines.

Roads become less wide, less complicated. Two lanes up over rolling hills or down. Hills become bigger hills, then mountains. One mountain we tunnel through; I'm anxious in the long darkness. Only forward and back in a tunnel. No side exits.

I exhale once I see the light-filled blue sky. The open road.

Driving, driving, driving some more. There are few cars, mostly semitrucks carrying new cars, oil, and logs. The radio plays static.

Buildings have shrunk and disappeared. Huge Christmas-like trees pierce the sky. At their roots, there's wilted, crackling scrub, dry bushes.

"Why's everything brown?"

"Drought," says the driver. His blue eyes crinkle, looking back at me through the rearview mirror. "When you map, you've got to note the landscape, too. Might save your life."

How'd he know I was mapping?

"She's drawing mazes," pipes Nessa, blinking sleepy eyes.

"Map. Maze. What's the difference?" Kelvin asks.

"A maze is like a map," answers Jamie, turning around in her seat. "Both give a bird's-eye view.

But maps can be simpler—from here to there. A maze is a puzzle. It's not always clear which path is best."

"Isn't that true for maps?" asks Jay, sitting beside me.

"No, the most useful maps are grounded in reality. Mazes can be real, too. Made from hedges in a garden. Mostly, though, they're artificial, imaginary."

"Don't forget, maps can have streams, valleys, mountains," calls the driver. "Topography. It keeps you from getting lost."

Topography. No one wants to admit they don't know what it means.

"Leo's razzing you," laughs Jamie. "You'll find out about it when we go hiking. Ridges, valleys, altitudes. Won't she, Dylan?"

"Maybe," answers Dylan, not looking back. "Not everybody is good in the outdoors."

Jay tenses, defensive.

I wonder: *How do you show altitude on a flat map?*

In the rearview mirror, Leo winks at me. "This is a talented group."

"The best," says Jamie, cheerful.

Dylan mutters. (The windshield swallows his words.)

Nessa taps Jay's clasped hands. She smiles; he relaxes.

I flip through my notebook. For the Bronx, I've got all kinds of maps. Streets and corners. How to get in, get out. Left, straight, right. But the Bronx doesn't have this rough terrain, these concrete roads and rolling hills.

Pressing my face closer to the window, I'm not sure where we're going. It bothers me.

Clouds fade; the sun is setting. The sky is so big.

I never knew there were so many trees. The Bronx is all buildings. Telephone wires. Streetlights. Signs. And people—thousands and thousands of people.

Now I feel like I'm disappearing into a horror movie. All the people have vanished. Replaced by monster trees.

Leo revs the engine. He's older than Jamie and Dylan—like he could be their dad. Maybe granddad?

If Bibi were here, she'd say, "*Mr.* Leo. Call your elders mister. Or ma'am."

Yet with his rolled-up plaid sleeves, gray hair, and beard, Mr. Leo seems just Leo. More relaxed than grown-ups in the Bronx. Jamie and Dylan smile at him like he's their friend. Leo looks like a neighbor man who remembers every kid's birthday and dresses up like Santa for the Salvation Army.

The van purrs, rumbles. Sunlight bakes us. Everyone dozes. Dylan slumps against the window. Jamie slumps against him. Jay's head tilts straight back. Even DeShon is sound asleep, though his headset still buzzes. Nessa and A'Leia, bodies twisted, hands tucked beneath their heads, are slightly smiling while they're dreaming.

I don't sleep. Only Leo and I are awake. From time to time, he looks back at me. His eyes, with

arching thick brows above, study me. (Like Nessa
did on the plane.)

It's like he can tell I'm different.

I can't shake the feeling that Leo knows something about me that I don't know.

Odd. He's waiting for me to reveal—what?

More oddly, Leo reminds me of Bibi. Both of
them watching, waiting for me to do something I
can't even dream about.

Like I've got magic buried inside me.

I shiver.

Maybe I do?

III

Evening. There's a spotlight on a wooden sign with red letters:

WILDERNESS ADVENTURES

Engine groaning up the steep driveway, the van slows, stopping on gravel. Leo yells excitedly: "We're here!"

I step into the dry, crisp air. Up ahead, I see a brightly lit, one-story house. Smoke rises from a chimney. (I don't like fireplaces.) The cool night air soothes.

Me, Nessa, and Jay don't move. Who knew

night air could be so different? Bracing, smelling of green, cedar, and smoke.

"I like it," says Nessa. Me and Jay know what she means. Jay stretches. Nessa twirls, happy.

"Kelvin, A'Leia," Dylan shouts, "let's unload the van." DeShon, the biggest of all of us (even Leo and Dylan), stands like a statue.

Jay pitches in, dragging suitcases. Nessa joins him.

My mind starts mapping the space. To the right, about ten feet from the main building, are four cabins scattered six feet apart. To the far left are a large barn and a grass pen. There's only thick darkness beyond the buildings.

I frown, worried the driveway is the only EXIT.

Jamie hands each of us a flashlight. Pebbles, not concrete, crackle beneath my feet.

"Welcome to Paradise Ranch," Leo booms, proudly. "Your summer home."

Dinner is chili and biscuits. Afterward, we separate into cabins. Nessa is my roommate. We don't say much. But Nessa reminds me of the girls from home. Easy, relaxed around me.

The cabin is simple. Two twin beds. A dresser to share. A nightstand with a lamp. No central heat or air-conditioning.

I stare uncomfortably at the fireplace. A grate holds logs; a mesh screen locks the fire in. Flames—yellow, orange, and red—spiral upward.

"It's beautiful," says Nessa.

Awful beautiful, I think. If I stare too long at the flames, I'll remember what I most want to forget. I slip into bed, my back to the fire.

"Night," I say.

"Glad you're my roomie," Nessa answers softly.

Her words make me feel good.

I pull the quilt over my head, murmuring a prayer for my parents, for Bibi, who gave up everything to raise me.

I tell myself, "Don't dream."

Where am I?

The bed is hard, the pillow flat.

There're no kitchen sounds. No Bibi opening, shutting cupboards and shuffling silverware. No bacon smells. Or warming toast.

No Bibi yelling, "Adaugo, wake up. See the world."

Strange, this wild darkness soothes. No sirens or honking cars. No shouts outside the window. No streetlight or neon glare. Not even the dull glow from my *Black Panther* night-light.

My morning pattern is broken. It's disturbing. I should be scared.

Then I remember: Wilderness Adventures.

I'm in California.

I swing my legs down. The cabin is cold. The floor colder. Only embers glow in the fireplace. Uneasy, I look away, wishing I didn't still smell smoke.

Nessa softly snores. She must've fallen asleep gazing at the fire.

Gray ash collects on the grate; black burns scar logs.

The fire is nearly dead. Good.

Good sign, too, I didn't dream.

A fresh start?

I quickly dress—jeans, socks, shoes, T-shirt, and hoodie. I tiptoe, opening the door.

I'm surprised it's still so dark. Stars sparkle like fireworks thrown across the sky. The Bronx only has distant, small stars. What time is it?

I never knew the night sky could be so amazing—trillions of blinking, sparkling, spinning lights in a velvet-black sky. Some stars streak like soft lightning.

But it's the trees that take my breath away. Looking out from the ranch instead of toward it, it's impossible to miss I'm deep inside a forest.

Trees, thousands and thousands, forty, fifty (maybe more) feet tall. I feel like I'm in a movie, in *The Lord of the Rings*. Next to the trees, the buildings seem like Lincoln Log toys. Not all the trees are the same. Some have leaves, some needles. Some are lean, upright, like stakes. Others stretch wide and deep into the ground, their roots seeming like legs and feet. They're all towering, magical. Maybe there *are* Ents, like Treebeard? *"Come and see. Come and see."* The forest is calling me, inviting me to explore.

"I figured you'd be the first up."

The sound startles me. A shadow, swinging a lantern, edges closer. The lantern rises; Leo's face glows.

When it's dark in the Bronx, I'm careful about strangers. But Leo seems a perfect fit here. His wrinkled face, his relaxed and swinging arms. His beard quivers when he smiles.

"There's always one."

"One what? A Black kid?"

"No, I mean a city kid. A kid who didn't know they belonged in the wild."

I want to say something smart, sassy. I hear

Bibi: *"Get out of your own way, Adaugo. Just be."* I exhale.

"We'll wake the others at dawn," says Leo.

"What time is it?"

"Four."

"In the morning?"

"Not so bad. You're still on East Coast time. Besides, this is the best time of day." He hesitates. "Feel it, do you?"

You sound like Bibi, I think. The quieter his voice, the more important his words seem.

Leo's right. Being outdoors feels good. No crowds, loud sounds, or police and ambulance sirens. Like the world went back in time. Though I've never seen one, I think I hear an owl. There's a steady *whoosh* of wind rustling through the bushes and trees. It feels special to be up when everyone else is sleeping—like they're missing out and I'm—what?

"Alive?" Leo smiles.

I'm shocked. He knew what I was thinking even before I did. I do feel alive, like I'm shaking off old skin. Morning darkness is exciting. I inhale deep.

"Better than a flashlight." Leo hands me a lantern. He walks toward the trees, then whistles, high-pitched. A shadow with white streaks races out of the woods. My heart races, scared. A wild animal?

"It's just Ryder."

Tongue lolling, bright, beady eyes—I swear this dog grins.

"Sit."

Ryder sits, his gaze never leaving mine.

In the Bronx, there aren't many dogs. (For most, it's one mouth too many to feed.) Our neighbor, Mr. Bailey, owns a beagle. He cleans its poop off the street. Says owners who don't "give dogs a bad name." Ms. Patel carries her beloved Chihuahua in a purse.

Ryder is big. If he stood on two legs, he'd be as tall as me.

"He's an Australian Shepherd. Smart." Leo lowers his lantern.

Ryder has one black eye, one blue. Weird.

"To the barn."

Ryder's nose pushes my thigh. I step back. He barks, pushes me again.

"He's herding you," Leo chuckles. "No sheep here. But he's decided you'll do."

I extend my hand.

"Palm up," says Leo. "That way he knows you're a friend."

Ryder sniffs my hand.

"Can I pet him?"

"Ask him."

"Can I pet you?" Amazingly, Ryder shoves his head beneath my hand. I stroke his fur.

Barking, he spins, trotting ahead. I follow him, feeling safe, happier than in a long, long time.

Every few feet, Ryder stops and looks back, waiting for me.

We pass cabins. Jay, DeShon, Kelvin, and A'Leia are still asleep like Nessa.

Leo's boots crunch, kick up dust. Broad-shouldered but not much taller than me, he talks while he walks. A dim sliver of blue glows through the trees.

"It's morning twilight. The sun is beneath the horizon. When the sun crests, clouds and sky will shine, glimmering orange-yellow."

Who knew?

"Sun rises in the east. Sets in the west." His blunt fingers are pointing. "So, where's north?" He stops, peering at me.

I don't know. In the Bronx, street signs have N or S or E or W. What does it matter where's north?

"Think."

I scrunch my lips. Ryder sits, watching me.

I think of my maps, all the maps I've ever seen. Sometimes there's a compass or arrows pointing N, S, E, or W.

"If west is in front," I murmur, "north is to the right. East behind you."

Leo nods. "Smart girl. A mapmaker, better than anyone, should know which way to go."

"So I can escape," I blurt.

Leo's head tilts. Funny, Ryder's ears perk; his head tilts, too.

"Interesting. Most people just don't want to be lost."

A morning breeze stirs arounds us. Darkness is lifting.

Leo's curious about me. Not like the school psychologist, Ms. Cunningham. She always wants me to talk about feelings:

"Hard being an orphan, isn't it? What do you remember most about your parents? What do you remember most about that night? How do you feel, Addy?"

All her questions—dumb, dumb. DUMB.

Leo doesn't say anything, doesn't judge. Just waits.

Emotions swirl. If I cry, will darkness hide my tears?

He whistles for Ryder and strides toward the barn. Leo guessed my sadness.

"I bought this land," he calls over his shoulder.

I blink, scurry until I'm beside him. "This is yours?"

"Yes, I own it. Much as anyone can."

"All of it? Everything I see?"

"Even some you can't. Far off, into the forest, land stretches for miles."

"Can I draw it?"

"For escaping?"

Looking away from his gaze, I keep walking.

"May and Belle are waiting," says Leo.

"Who?"

"My cows."

"Yours?"

"Yes. Horses. Chickens, too. Everything belongs to me. And Ryder. Isn't that right, boy? Of course, maybe I belong to him and he thinks those are his chickens. Hard to say."

Ryder barks.

"I thought you were the driver."

"I'm whatever is needed. Ranch boss, stable boy, teacher." He pauses. "Wilderness Adventures was my idea. I was a city kid once."

I'm unsettled. I'm good at figuring out people. But I didn't guess Leo's other selves. He acts low-key, calm, not like a boss.

"Every now and then—a kid reminds me of me."

"Me?" I scowl. I'm nothing like him. He's nothing like me. He's richer than me and Bibi. Maybe he's got more money than all the folks in the Bronx? He doesn't live in a broken-down high-rise apartment. Even his animals have houses.

"Wilderness for city kids. You mean poor kids. Wilderness for poor kids. I can't remind you of you. You were never as poor as me."

"No, I wasn't."

"See. We're not the same. You make yourself feel good helping poor kids. Who needs it? We've got ice cream trucks on the avenue, Stop & Shops, trees in Bronx Park. What else does anyone need?"

Ryder, feeling my distress, pushes his head against my hand.

Leo watches me, not pityingly, not disrespect-ful. With kindness, even a little amusement. "Yup. We don't have any Popsicles. But we've got Eagle's Ridge.

"Ryder," he yells. "Get the pack."

Ryder runs toward the barn, grips a backpack with his teeth, dragging it to Leo.

"Good boy," Leo pats his head. To me, he says, "Never venture unprepared. I always keep a pack with emergency supplies."

I stare blankly.

"You'll learn. Water, food, first aid." He steps closer. "Here. An extra flashlight. You ready?" He's daring me, and before I can reply, he turns, saying emphatically, "The Lookout."

"Follow in my steps."

I try to place my feet where his land. But Leo walks fast; it's hard to keep up. He knows when the trail dips, when it rises, how to avoid branches, rocks, leap over boulders.

The trail seems endless. It's steadily going uphill, higher and higher. I'm gasping to keep up. Leo's flashlight is steady, shining straight ahead. My light zigzags right, left, up, down. Focusing on the trail, it's hard to keep my hand steady.

This is a test. To see if I'll give up. In the Bronx, it's trading insults. *Snap!* Playing the dozens, rapping and rhyming to see who'll back down first. Who'll get too angry (fistfighting angry). Who'll break into tears.

Here, it's not emotional, it's physical. My legs

are tight, aching. There's a cramp in my side. I'm sweating, though the darkness is cool. I unzip my hoodie.

Leo, carrying a pack, never seems tired or out of breath.

Ears flat, Ryder races; he's so happy.

We hike for what feels like hours. I wonder if Nessa and the others will be awake soon. Will they miss me?

I fall into rhythm, watching Leo's back and pack dodging through trees. Ryder keeps darting ahead, then dashes back to us. Each time, Leo says, "Good boy." I start saying it, too, "Good boy."

Leo stops; I stumble against him. He steadies me. "Look. Eagle Ridge."

We stand on a hill seeing a huge ridge that extends miles south of us, rising in the mist. Dawn is just reaching out to it across the valley below.

"It's amazing."

So many textures—prickly pines, rough,

crackling wood, smooth leaves, velvet brush cover, and weeds and dirt.

I can see how mountains create valleys, how the hills make depressions and rises. Nothing is truly level. Not even the stream southeast of us, snaking a path over and between fallen logs, stones, and rocks.

"Farther east, miles away, the stream becomes a river and creates a waterfall."

"I've never seen a waterfall."

"What do you think of this?" Leo sweeps his hand through the air, like he's a magician conjuring a world.

Landscapes. I've seen them in books, paintings. But I've never *felt* one before. Never felt how the earth existed long, long, long before I was born. The beauty rocks me.

In school, they talk about the environment. "Save Mother Earth." "Go Green." "Stop Climate Change." "Reuse or Refuse." "Lend a Hand, Plant a Tree." "Don't Pollute."

Here, now, I glimpse ancient shapes of growing trees, ferns, rolling hills and mountains. Glimpse how ages ago and even now, water brushes, curving and carving the land.

Buildings don't block my view. I can see for miles. Miles upon miles.

"Think you can map this?"

My breath catches. Excited, my fingers twitch, itching for pencils.

Leo's blue eyes gaze into my brown.

"I grew up surrounded by concrete and brick, crowded freeways. People everywhere in cars, on buses, subways, trains." He's talking to me serious. "Nothing wrong with city life. But I always felt lost."

"I'm not lost."

"No. You just draw escape paths."

"You don't know anything about me." Heat rushes through me. *I see fire in the main house, fire in my cabin, fire in...* No, I won't remember. Won't dream. Hands clenching, I shut my eyes.

"Look, Addy—Adaugo."

"You know my full name?" I ask. Of course he knows my name. Bibi wrote it on the application.

"Look." Leo is beside me. We're standing, our shoulders almost touching.

Leo breathes deep, slow. In through his nose, out through his mouth. My breath starts to match, mimic his as I keep gazing at rocks, the winding stream. Staring at thick, twisted tree roots, I scan upward, seeing green extending higher, glowing against craggy granite and rock. The backdrop is a brightening sky with flamelike streaks bursting from the sunrise.

The horizon is haunting. Stunning.

Grandma Bibi loves talking about the African wild—the national parks, elephants, antelopes, gazelles, mangrove swamps, rain forests, and savannahs. Most times I didn't pay much attention. Living in the city, I couldn't imagine a differing landscape.

Bibi left Nigeria to care for me when my parents died. I didn't understand her loss. Until now. Bibi must've known I needed this.

Leo did, too.

"How'd you know?"

He knows what I'm asking. His hand touches my shoulder. "Intuition. Most folks think the environment they're born into is the only way to live.

You never know until you've been somewhere, seen something different."

A shriek pierces the air.

"An eagle."

It's the largest, most graceful bird I've ever seen. It soars upward, then glides. Then, quick, it alters course. Flying toward us.

"A bald eagle. But it's not really bald."

It's coming closer, closer. "Feathers. White feathers on its head."

"Female. Coming in to look at us. Must have a nest."

"She's huge."

Another shriek. The eagle extends its wings. Six, seven, at least eight feet wide. Wider than people are tall.

"Don't see this in the city."

"No." I exhale. "She's beautiful." This is the first live eagle I've ever seen.

"Another reason I thought you were a wilderness spirit."

"Why?"

"*Adaugo.* I googled it. It's Nigerian. Means 'daughter of an eagle,' right?"

The eagle abruptly turns, heads westward, flaps its wings, rising higher; then it dives. Hidden by trees.

"The eagle is a powerful spirit animal in many cultures. German, Mexican, Native peoples—"

"Bibi tells me in Nigeria, there used to be a festival in an eagle sanctuary. Most of the eagles have disappeared, so there's no celebration anymore."

"Everywhere, eagles need protecting. From us, from people.

"The wilderness—rain forests, deserts, Arctic tundra—need protecting, too. Fuels like coal, oil, and gas make the world hotter. See here?" Leo pats a tree trunk. His fingers flick, and bark crackles, falls. "Drought stresses it. Makes it vulnerable to fire.

"Bark beetles make it worse. Warming causes baby booms. Used to be one generation, now it's two, three generations a year. Thousands of beetles laying eggs, spreading bacteria, and killing trees."

My hand scrapes the bark. Spiders scurry between cracks. But it's the black beetles that relentlessly chew.

"Because of climate change, half of Earth's forests are gone."

How can that be? So much beauty lost. How can we keep it? Save it?

Again, the eagle glides toward us.

"Welcome home."

My heart swells. The morning sun hovers above the horizon.

I swear—the eagle tips its wing. I see its eye looking at me.

DISCOVERY

Hiking boots. Leo, Jamie, and Dylan arrange them side by side by size.

"Ugly," says A'Leia. "Heavy, too." DeShon doesn't say anything. He isn't happy leaving his headphones in the cabin.

Me, Jay, and Nessa sit on the ground, struggling with the rigid boots.

Kelvin and A'Leia, standing, keep trying to shove their toes inside like the boots are slippers. Amazing, DeShon, crouching, balancing his right foot on his knee, slips his boot on just fine.

"Side mesh," says Jamie, "makes the boots breathable."

"Breathable? They're A-L-I-V-E," Jay cackles as if the boots were Frankenstein.

Dylan scowls. "Not funny."

"Circulating air keeps your feet dry." Leo flips a boot. "The rubber sole helps you grip the terrain."

"Why's the toe and heel so hard?" asks Nessa.

"So you don't stub your toe against rocks?" asks Jay.

"Right. And the heel helps stabilize your foot. But the best part is your pack." Leo passes out backpacks with a side pocket holding a metal water bottle.

"Inside, some jerky—"

"Nasty," pipes DeShon, scrunching his nose. "Dried beef."

Jamie tosses a protein bar. "You might like this better."

"Why snacks?" asks Nessa. "We're just going for a walk."

"A hike," insists Leo.

Nessa shrugs. "What's the difference?"

* * *

A walk might be twenty, thirty minutes. A hike can take hours.

I love every minute. (Loved it ever since me and Leo hiked The Lookout.)

We've fallen into line. Jamie leading, me behind her. Trailing me are Jay, Kelvin, A'Leia, Nessa, and DeShon. Dylan's in the rear. Nobody talks, just moves—feet sliding, shuffling, stomping.

Kelvin pants; A'Leia puffs. I can't hear DeShon's or Nessa's breathing. But I suspect they're struggling a bit, too.

Me and Jay are solid—breathing deep, but not harsh or rushed.

The pack makes me stand straighter, shoulders down, pulled back. I mirror Jamie: arms loose, knees bent slightly, planting your boots solid. Going downhill, she shortens her step, keeps centered, not leaning forward.

Hiking is an art. I'm not escaping; instead, I'm

following a new trail. Following the rhythm and sound of boots.

I wish Leo and Ryder were here. But they stayed behind. I smile, remembering Ryder hopping on his hind legs, his front paws clawing the air, and Leo, hands on hips, nodding, encouraging me. All of us.

"Where does our hike end?" asks Jay.

"Oasis Circle," Jamie answers.

My eyes scan the scenery: never-ending trees, massive boulders, fallen logs. A soft cushion of ground cover except where it's been worn away by boots.

"Keep on the trail," Jamie warns. "Limit our impact on the forest."

If we stray, will there be fewer birds singing? Or more? Fewer smells of bright, alive green and decomposing wood? Or more?

Jamie stops, stoops, waves for us to close in. "See these holes?"

Everyone except DeShon stares. Kelvin and

A'Leia take off their glasses. I realize they're both nearsighted.

"A rabbit warren. Underground are passage-ways and burrows."

My mind maps. I blink, imagining complex tunnels.

"And above, see the holes in that tree trunk?" asks Dylan. "Woodpeckers."

We all look up.

"There's a nest inside the hole."

Jay exclaims, "Branches create a roof."

It's true. Branches crisscross, making it hard to see sky.

"Great observation, Jay," mutters Dylan.

I frown. I sense Dylan's mocking Jay. Why?

"They're fighting for the light," says Jamie.

"Makes the forest cool," answers Nessa. "I like it."

"Still, there's a struggle," argues Jay. "Nature, like people, fights to survive. I never thought about it before. Nature, you know, is just *there*."

Jamie nods. "Let's keep moving."

We hike on—our steps loud, uneven. Even though it's cooler in the forest, it's still hot. Sweat bubbles on DeShon's face, streams down Kelvin's neck. A'Leia's varsity jacket is tied to her pack.

Jay's right. But Leo taught me forests struggle mostly because of people. Doesn't seem fair. When did a forest hurt anybody?

Glittering light, like diamonds, peeks through branches, dark and green leaves.

"I want to go back," complains DeShon. "My feet hurt."

"You speak," Jamie answers, teasing.

"This is stupid. I get it. Nature. We don't have to stay out all day."

"This is the adventure," quips Jay. "If you're not down with it, why'd you come?"

DeShon's face is grim.

"One more mile," adds Dylan. "Once we reach Oasis Circle, we can head back."

"Back?"

"What did you think, DeShon?" Jay asks, exasperated.

"I'm dead tired."

"Addy's been tearing it up. You can't keep up with a girl?"

"Yeah," sasses Nessa. "Girls are just as good as guys."

"Better," hollers A'Leia. "Right?"

Kelvin nods.

"Addy, you've been getting down. Representing city kids great. We should at least try to be as good as you."

Jay means well, but now DeShon is upset with me.

"Okay, let's break," orders Dylan. "Hiking isn't arguing."

"Eat, rest. We'll all feel better," says Jamie.

Me, Jay, Nessa, Kelvin, and A'Leia sit on the ground, making a circle. We dump our snacks in the center and everyone picks what they like best. Trail mix, raisins.

"Really, Jay? Jerky?"

"Always wanted to try it. Feel like a caveman," he grunts, as his teeth rip the bag.

Kelvin picks up the package. "Smoked. Nasty stuff."

Jay shrugs. "Tastes good to me."

Not eating, DeShon sits apart, his shoulders rounded. I can tell he really is tired.

Nessa taps my knee. "You're good at hiking."

"I like it."

"Me too," mumbles Jay, still chewing.

We all smile. Except DeShon.

Jay's strong. He likes being capable, athletic. If we were in trouble, he'd be a good person to count on.

DeShon is more closed off. Music comforts him, but even though he's bigger than Jay—bigger than all of us—he's weak, out of shape.

Pushing his glasses back on the bridge of his nose, Kelvin says, "Nature's amazing. It's better than a park. Way better than my apartment building surrounded by gravel and weeds."

"Way better." A'Leia mimics him, sliding her glasses over her nose.

"A'Leia, you got a boyfriend?" Nessa blurts.

A'Leia blushes.

"Oops, I'm sorry. I didn't mean to embarrass you. You're always wearing or carrying that varsity jacket. I thought—"

"I'm A'Leia's new best friend," laughs Kelvin. "Friends are better than a boyfriend, girlfriend. So a guy gives you his varsity jacket. How many good-looking guys wear glasses? Understand not seeing distance well?" Kelvin's palm shades his eyes; he juts his head, pretending to see far, far away. "It's a tree. Yes, definitely a tree.

"Right, A'Leia?"

"Right," she giggles, her index finger pushing her glasses higher.

Kelvin and A'Leia smile. Like twins. Or brother and sister. Similar on the *inside*, not the outside.

"Addy, you're not even sweating," says Jay. "What's your secret?"

(Since when do I give advice?)

"I watch Jamie," I say, standing, demonstrating. "Keep your body upright, tight. Everything else loose."

"Do you always pay close attention to everything?" asks Jay. "Surroundings? People?"

Feeling shy, I duck my head. I *do* pay attention.

"That's why I'm going to follow Addy," proclaims Nessa. "She pays attention, draws maps. If there's trouble, I'm following her."

Nessa means it. I can't help feeling a little bit proud.

"Let's go. Trash in your backpack. Leave only footprints," exclaims Jamie.

We all clean up (except DeShon).

Staring, Jay stands in front of him.

"Again," hollers Nessa. "Squaring off. So stupid."

Jamie and Dylan are trying to hide they're watching us. Usually I'm the only one out of place. Here, everyone is.

I speak up. "DeShon, what kind of music do you like?"

"Rap, R&B"—he grins, looking almost handsome—"and salsa."

"You dance?" asks Nessa.

DeShon shakes his head.

"Gonna change that. Tonight," insists Nessa, moving her hips and feet, stepping forward and back.

Smiling, DeShon picks up his trash.

"Let's go," calls Jamie. "Dylan will lead now. I'll bring up the rear."

"Okay," squeals Nessa, having fun, doing a combination hike-dance up the hill.

We all fall into a straight line again. I'm behind happy Nessa. Jay's right behind me. I notice he's bending his knees, keeping his arms loose.

Kelvin, A'Leia, and DeShon follow.

"It's only another mile," insists Dylan. "You can make it."

Ten minutes later, Kelvin is breathing heavily. Too heavily. We all hear him.

I poke Jay. We both see A'Leia, angry, encouraging, whispering, giving Kelvin water.

Jay shrugs.

The mile is hard, not because it's long but because the ground is hard. Cracked dry.

We all step unevenly over shriveled branches, fallen logs. Shade isn't enough. Everybody's sweating now. Nessa trudges like the rest of us. Kelvin's breath is more even.

"We're here."

"Here." Jamie echoes Dylan.

"Here? Oasis Circle?" asks Kelvin.

No one answers. We don't have to. So beautiful, we probably wouldn't have minded hiking another five miles.

Oasis Circle is a clearing, a nearly perfect circle of green ground cover and trees rising at least sixty feet, protecting it. But the trees don't make a canopy; rather, the sky is open and sun shines like God's or an angel's light.

"It's like a church," says Kelvin, awestruck.

Jay steps close behind me, murmuring, "I've never felt so safe."

I understand. Us six kids and Jamie and Dylan all fit comfortably inside the circle. Everyone's face is upraised toward the sun. Even DeShon is awestruck.

I think, *The hike has brought us closer together.*

"Look," shouts Jay.

An eagle, light behind its wings, is circling above. It glides around and around—three times—then soars high like it's going to burst the sun.

"That was weird," says Nessa.

"That was grace," Bibi would say. I can imagine Leo nodding, adding, "A wilderness spirit."

Funny yet cool, I think my grandmother and Leo could be friends.

Dinnertime, we all shovel food. Grilled fish with rice. Headless, cut in half. Salt and pepper. Parsley and lemon on the side.

Jay swallows, mutters, "Best thing I ever ate."

Our table is long wood, a fancy picnic table. A'Leia reaches for another helping of rice.

None of us has eaten trout. "Wish it was blackened catfish," says Nessa, still chowing down.

DeShon groans. He's too tired to share music. Or even dance. "Blisters on my feet," he complains. "Unbelievable."

"Man, put your foot down." Kelvin slaps his toe. "You stink."

DeShon grumbles, but he lowers his foot. Squeezes lemon on his fish.

Behind me, at their own table, are Jamie and Dylan. Both wear jeans and plaid shirts. They're both thin but strong. Outdoor strong. Not like weight lifters in the Bronx.

They're chattering about dreams. "I want to be an environmental engineer. Or else a climatologist."

"Where do you go to school?" asks Dylan.

"UC Davis."

"I'm Santa Cruz."

"Tuition's expensive."

"Tell me about it."

"This job is so much better than cashiering in the grocery store."

"Last summer, I worked changing tires. I was inside, every day, smelling rubber all the time and tightening lug nuts. I graduate next year. I'm going to apply to be a park ranger. I only took this job because I want Leo's recommendation. People say he's got sway with the Park Service."

Engineers build. An environmental engineer? Not sure what they do. Or a climatologist, either. What does either do, exactly? Park ranger sounds strange. Zion, a guy at school, has a brother who's an Army Ranger. He says they're the best soldiers in the world. Do park rangers "lead the way," too?

I've never heard of these jobs. Never knew references were needed for a job. Thought you just filled out an application.

Now I know why Dylan (though he tries to hide it) isn't always thrilled to be with us. Is it because we're city kids? Black kids? Or just kids?

Jamie's nice. I might like her college. UC Davis. (I'll find it on a map.)

"Heard you all did good." At the head of the table, Leo's smiling, proud like we're all his kids. "Not easy to hike five miles."

"Exhausting," says A'Leia.

"But fun," Jay crows.

"Great," says Leo, patting his shoulder. "You'll be doing twenty miles in no time."

DeShon chokes, spitting out green beans. Jay, Kelvin, and Nessa laugh.

"Gross," says A'Leia, nose crinkling. She covers the half-chewed green beans with a napkin.

Twenty miles. My mind starts mapping the distance. Today it took almost four hours. How long for twenty? Longer than a day. I think I can do it. No, I want to do it. I can do it.

Hike twenty miles. Maybe more.

Wow. Twenty miles a day, I'd have to hike much faster.

How fast, how many miles can I go?

II

Me and Nessa enter our cabin. The fireplace is roaring with wood crackling, logs shifting and bursting with yellow-red flames. I've learned Leo sets the cabin fires, placing logs, positioning grates.

I'd rather be outside in the cold. Except Nessa would ask questions. Think I'm crazy.

We slip into our pajamas.

My back to the fire, I sit on the edge of the bed, opening my binder.

I draw a square room—one door out, two windows. Just like me and Bibi's apartment.

Just like (I think) the apartment I lived in before. A memory stirs. Another apartment. Before

Bibi. Where I lived with my parents. My hand trembles. The pencil smudges, wriggles the lines. Heart beating fast, I keep drawing arrows, possible paths to **ESCAPE**.

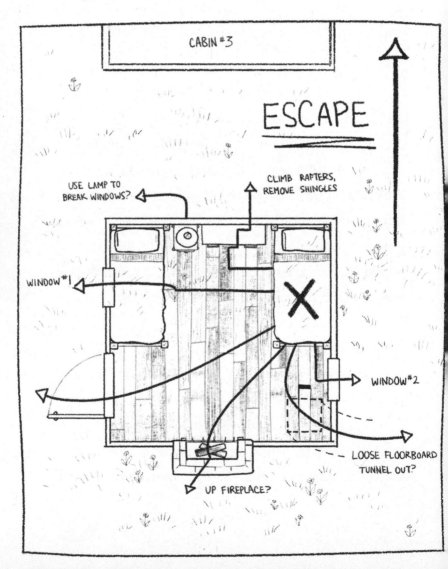

Though I keep redrawing paths, there aren't enough exits.

Turning, I see Nessa still facing the fire. Her body's limp, her arm dangling off the bed. She's sound asleep.

I stare at the flame, feeling a new urgency to draw maps—how to leave the cabin, the ranch. Still at the forest's edge, facing wilderness, I won't know which way to go.

I panic. My mistake.

I let myself forget. I should've been looking for guideposts, how to escape. Not just blindly following Jamie, following somebody else's trail.

I stopped paying attention. Rabbit warrens, woodpeckers are nice, but without a trail would I be able to find my way back? If I *needed* to go back?

I can't breathe.

Oasis Circle—what if I needed to get there? To be safe?

Coming and going, arrival and departure... remaining, escaping... going toward and away. Thoughts jumble my mind.

I think of the eagle soaring. I need to see everything. I need to know where to run, where to hide...where to stay. Where to fly.

Escape. Flee. From what?

My mind answers, "Fire."

I'm sleeping on a daybed. A yellow blanket covering me and my cloth doll, Maya.

Maya is my best friend.

I'm four. A big girl.

Hanging from the cracked ceiling are light bulbs with slow, twirling blades. Smoke spreads, spiraling outward.

I hear insistent whispers, scuffling. "Smother it." Mama's voice. "Smother it."

Across from me and Maya, Mama and Pop's bed is empty. We all sleep, eat, cook in one big room.

There's a wild clang. Metal rattles. A bang. Mama screams.

Shivering, gripping Maya, I sit up. See Mama swatting a frying pan of flames with a dish towel.

Pop stomps his feet. Flaming grease flies. Tiny flames dot the carpet.

Mama screams again. I scream.

I push back against the wall. Smoke floats down. There's no place to go.

Coughs, crying. More coughs. I cover me and Maya with the blanket. If I don't see the flames, maybe they'll disappear. But I feel them. Searing, suffocating heat.

"Mama."

"Adaugo."

Pop screams, long, low, guttural.

Gasping, crying, I wake. Nightmares from the Bronx won't leave me alone.

Thankfully, Nessa still sleeps. The fire in the fireplace should be dying, but it looks as if it's been sprayed with gas or more logs added. Is this really real?

Unsettled, I dress quickly, rush out the cabin.

"Ryder." He's sitting outside the door. Ears alert, head up.

Did Ryder know I needed comfort? How long has he been sitting, waiting for me?

Eyes sparkling, he's intensely watching my face. I drop to my knees, sobbing, wrapping my arms about his neck.

Ryder holds steady, rubs his head against my hair.

"You all right, Adaugo?"

I feel Ryder twisting his body and head to look at Leo. I'm not ready to look at him yet. Ryder's rising and falling chest, his heart beating, make me know I've stopped dreaming.

Like a big kid, Leo, legs crossed, sits on the ground. I can't help smiling.

Ryder relaxes, lying down between us.

"I've brought you this." A sketchpad. "And these." Pens and colored pencils held together with a rubber band. "You can draw the trails, Addy."

"Thank you." I flip to a blank page. I want to tell him what I think. But I'm nervous he'll think I'm complaining. I hear Bibi saying, *Truth-telling is healing.* Sometimes, though, I don't know what the truth is. I'm carrying a secret even I can't figure out. I just have instincts, warnings. A need to be prepared.

"Trails are just paths worn down and people, following them, over and over," I say. "Navigating off-path in the wild is different.

"Wilderness isn't like an apartment or building with windows and doors and hallways. It flows: rocks to brush to forest; stream to hills. No paths, no footsteps."

Ryder sits, snuffling. He knows I'm upset.

"There was a fire," I blurt. "My parents died. I survived. I don't remember how I did. I was a little kid. Bibi—"

"Your grandmother?"

"Says I'll remember my spirit's journey. Like me traveling here. She says the spirit takes journeys, too."

"You just need to get ready."

"Yes. You understand?"

I lean forward; Ryder shifts closer; Leo strokes Ryder.

"That's why you like maps."

"Yes. If I can see the layout, map it, I think I can always escape. Survive. Maybe I figured it out as a kid. Maybe my parents taught me, showed me how to escape earlier. I don't know. I was so little." My voice cracks, chokes. "Now there's only me and Bibi—she's old. Really, *really* old."

Leo knows what I'm trying to say. He nods.

I swallow. "My maps work in the Bronx. But I can't make them work here. No streets, corners. I can't plot my escape."

"You need to understand topographical maps."

He takes the sketchpad from me, slips a pencil from the rubber band. He puts two lanterns on the ground. The glow makes the paper shine.

"See. These are my property lines, the boundary where my land ends.

"Wilderness surrounds the camp. North is mountains. A range, miles deep and long. East is the ranch driveway, which gradually becomes a winding road, descending, leading to town, thirty

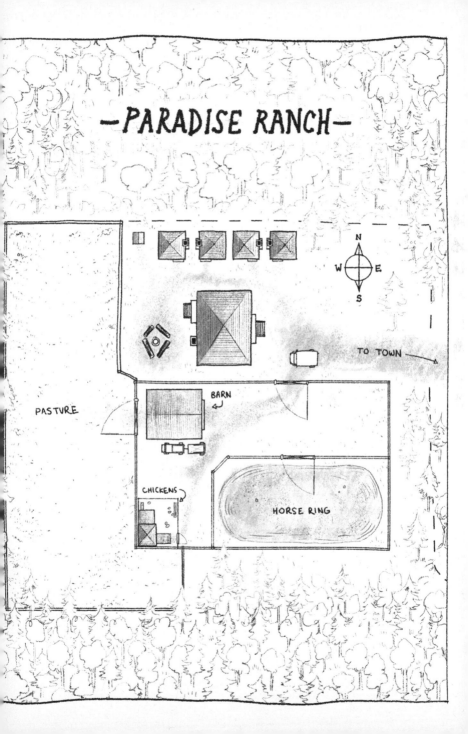

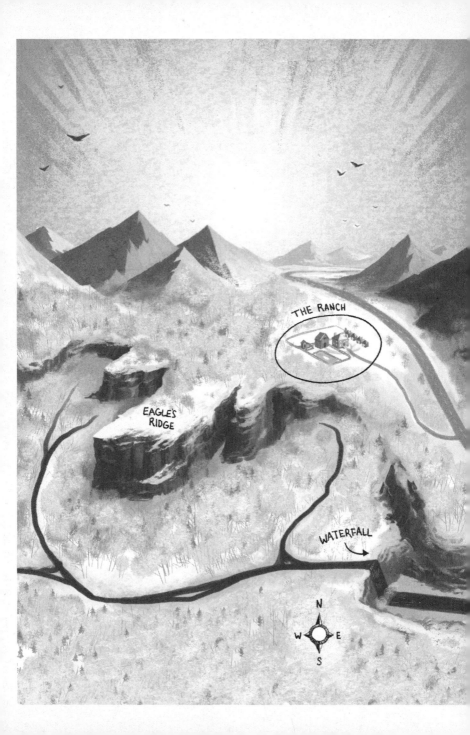

miles away. West is forest and more forest. South is Eagle's Ridge, and below it, a valley and a stream flowing east." He sketches rapidly. "Water plunges down a waterfall and creates a widening river. Two days out, the currents lead to another town.

"Cartography is making a map. Simple or complex."

Leo's good. As if we both were floating in the air, the land, buildings take shape. In the bottom right corner, he adds a compass, marking directions, N, S, E, and W.

"But that's all still flat. It doesn't show hills or how steep or how many steps there are. An escape route might look good on a flat map. But what if it turns into a cliff? Topography shows you elevations—how low is the valley, how high the hills and mountains, the length of creeks, streams.

"Here." He draws a square around Eagle's Ridge. On another page, he sketches the area, drawing nested arcs around Eagle's Ridge.

"We can also shade between the lines with colors.

"Green is for vegetation. Trees, bushes and

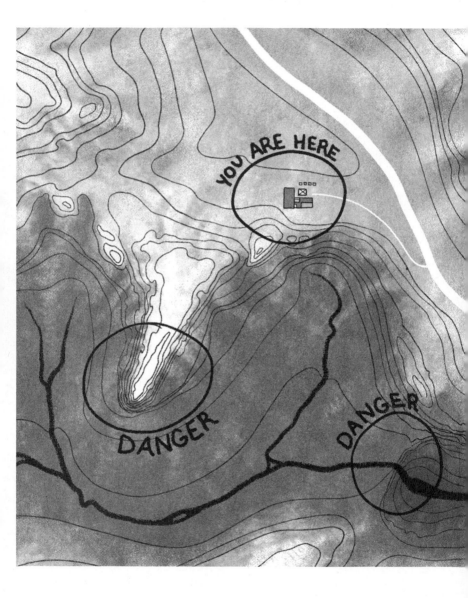

such. Blue for water. Dark and lighter brown for terrain. Lines can be straight or curved. Solid or dashed. Even a combination.

"How high, how steep is important."

He draws more contoured yet parallel lines.

"For elevation, Addy, count the number of curved lines above a point. Like this." The pencil tip points separately at each line. "Each line represents twenty feet."

"Four lines to here. Then five more. That's one hundred and eighty feet. Eagle's Ridge is the highest."

"That's right. If the lines are close together, it's steep; far apart, it's level. Here these lines are almost on top of each other. A sharp, sheer cliff before hitting the water. An eagle could soar down, pull up, and survive. But people—"

He doesn't have to say it. Falling off the cliff would mean death. Just like being trapped by a forest fire.

"This is why Bibi sent me to you. To teach me. She's always saying, 'New York isn't everywhere. Need to be prepared for other journeys.'"

"You're lucky. Bibi knew what you needed before you did. For most, it's hit or miss if they ever find their heart's landscape."

"You found it, didn't you?"

"I did." Then, more softly, adds, "Bibi must be a wilderness woman, too."

"She named me."

Leo chuckles. "Adaugo. Makes sense. No wonder you want to fly, see everything from on high.

"We'll go together."

"Where?"

"Eagle's Ridge. I'll teach you how to map it for yourself. But to really know it, you have to live it, go both on and off trails. Measure the height in steps. It's time-consuming.

"You might have to come back next summer, Addy. And the next. Maybe be a camp counselor.

"But first, breakfast."

Ryder's head pivots hearing, "breakfast."

I wonder—if I came here long enough, mapped every step and slope, would I feel safe?

III

Every day, outside my cabin while it's still chilly darkness, Ryder greets me. We go to the main house kitchen. Leo brews coffee. I fix Ryder his kibble. Sometimes, I fry him an egg. Ryder likes the yellow ooze.

While Ryder eats, Leo pours his coffee black. I add milk and sugar and act like I always drink coffee.

Four fifteen a.m. Like clockwork, we go to Leo's office, sit in front of his computer. On the wall are topographical maps: the world; the United States; the oceans, Earth, and moon. Pinned on the wall, too, is a picture of a tiny blond woman with a huge backpack. Smiling, she's waving at the person taking her photograph. Leo?

The office is cozy. A space heater warms us. Ryder naps. Me and Leo sit side by side, staring at light and colors radiating from the computer screen.

"Topographical maps show everything," I say, musing out loud. Nigeria has the Atlantic to the west. The Rivers Niger and Benue merge and make a Y shape.

Leo pokes the screen. "Instead of contour lines, the computer maps in three-D. See, to the south, nothing but lowlands. To the southeast, there's mountains. North, mainly plains.

"Its climate ranges from desert, to tropical, to equatorial—"

"Equatorial?"

"Near the equator. The center of the planet. It's a circle. Not a real one, but an imaginary divide between north and south. It's superhot. Closer to the sun than the North and South Poles."

Excitement growing, I look at Leo. "I never thought of mapping countries, our planet."

"Google Earth does it. Using satellites. Better than a plane or eagle view," he explains. "Aerial perspective makes everything smaller but allows you to see the whole. Seeing the whole is important to understand what's happening to our home. Look.

"Deforestation happens everywhere. But it's trees that clean carbon emissions and provide oxygen." Leo quickly taps the computer keys. "We need forests, but they're disappearing worldwide.

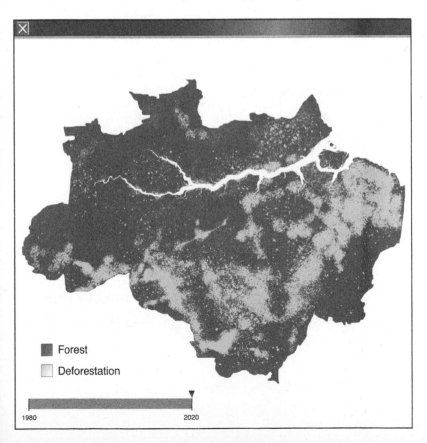

Forest

Deforestation

1980   2020

"Watch. It's a satellite image of the Amazon rain forest. Over two million acres, the planet's lungs. Yet more than twenty percent has been destroyed because of logging and wildfires."

I gasp. The video starts in 1980 and then, like a horrific, crazy race, the dates go up and the green on the map goes down. By 2020, HUGE parcels of land disappear.

The time-lapse film repeats again. All green, then specks, spots, square acres upon acres trans-form from green to brown.

"Climate change, Addy.

"Logging has gotten worse. As the planet warms, fires have become more horrendous. Right now, there are thousands of fires."

"Thousands?"

"Satellite maps tell the story. Look."

On the computer screen, red is overtaking green.

"September fifth is Amazon Rainforest Day. But so far this summer, sixty thousand fires have been detected. Fire season doesn't end until December."

My head hurts.

"Illegal deforestation makes it worse. Land that has been cleared for development—cattle grazing, clearing for lumber—increases the likelihood of burning. Another stress."

"Why doesn't someone stop it?"

"The Brazilian military tries. But most think the government should fund environmental groups. Soldiers aren't above being bribed."

Seeing the scale, seeing the satellite imagery make it real. Majestic trees are lost. What about the animals? The singing birds? Tiny insects? Aren't there monkeys and parrots in the Amazon? I feel bad that I don't know what other animals live in the Amazon forest. Or Bibi's African wild.

"So sad."

"Sometimes you need to see the whole to make sense of the world."

"I like seeing the whole." (*Like* is not the right word; it's also upsetting.)

"Of course you do. You're excellent at spatial reasoning."

"You mean it?" Except for Bibi, no one's ever told me I'm excellent at anything before.

"You can map in three-D, manipulate space. Engineers do it, surgeons do it. Mathematicians. Also architects and artists like Michelangelo."

(Who's Michelangelo?)

"Google Maps on a smartphone can be great. But in the wilderness, phones don't often work... so we use maps. The old-fashioned way. We...," he pauses, and I finish the sentence:

"Draw."

"And to draw...," he says dramatically.

"We need to explore."

This is the cue for Ryder to wake—for us to head outdoors. To wilderness. To the land beyond the ranch, beyond the trails. The land of my heart. The land of before time. Where Ryder remembers— maybe even dreams about where he once was wild?

"Wait, Leo. Can a satellite show me the flight path from New York to California?"

"Sure it can." Leo types. The computer screen flickers, showing a tiny plane arcing downward from New York City to Los Angeles. The image makes me feel good. When I fly home, I won't be flying blind. In my mind, I'll just reverse the flight path.

"Thanks, Leo."

He nods. *Understands me*, I think.

Worrying about the planet is scary. Maps make me feel in control. Like *seeing* might save me... help save the Earth.

Early every morning, me, Leo, and Ryder hike. It's special, important. Leo sends reports, maps to scientists tracking wildfires. Sundays, our trips take all day.

Mapping, I learn about paths, but I also learn about forest health: How dense are the trees? What kind? Are the trees diseased or dead? How many trunks have fallen or stand like an unlit match?

"Ryder, take us to New Land."

Ryder darts forward.

"New Land?"

"You'll see." Leo grins. "Go on, follow Ryder. I'll follow behind you."

Feels good following a dog. It's hot. I push aside low-hanging branches, step on weeds, grass, slips of bark. Wildflowers, yellow and white, clump together.

I inhale, deep. Smell's kind of funky but in a good way. Moist, deep. Like ancient times. Like maybe when wolves were becoming dogs.

Ryder's barking.

"Coming," I shout, then feel embarrassed. I forgot Leo was behind me. I sneak a peek. He's fallen back. Like he wants me to feel alone with Ryder. Feel the forest surrounding me.

I start jogging. "What is it, boy? What is it?" Smiling, I abruptly stop. I drop to my knees.

There's a jagged streak of black, burnt wood and ash-filled land. I can't tell where it ends. So strange, like a dragon or a flamethrower blazed a trail. But here, there, are green trees, upright and mighty.

Why would Leo want me to see this?

Hearing his steps, I don't look around. I'm angry. I don't know why. But I am.

"Sniff the shoots, Ryder. Sniff."

I look up. Leo's crazy.

"Watch Ryder."

Ryder's stepping gingerly, lowers his nose to the dirt. A green shoot like a curlicue pushes toward the light. He steps toward a scarred, dead log. Moss grows on it like a baby's blanket. Ryder sniffs a patch of tiny purple flowers. Then he pees on the roots of a baby bush. (Or is it a tree?)

Leo squats beside me. "We're going to map this. Show how the land is resurrecting."

"Resurrecting?"

"Renewing itself. Coming back from the dead."

"See the whole," I murmur. From on high, it would just look like the forest had an empty space, a misshapen wound snaking through thick growth. A close-up map can show the healing.

I stare, back and forth, at the reviving land, my blank page.

"Draw from the outside in. Untouched forest first. Then capture the scarred terrain."

"And the new growth?"

"Yes, the new growth. This may be our most detailed map yet."

I sketch, adding contours to capture the sloping land, trees, no trees, some rocks and boulders, collapsed logs. Here, there, I add green to signify shoots, new stalks, branches slowly, ever so slowly becoming baby trees.

"If we let it, Nature can thrive. Too bad it's not that easy for people."

Leo sounds like Bibi when she's talking about my mother. Her words are round-sounding but hollow. Sad like Leo's.

"Here, Ryder." He bounces over to me, sits, his front paws in the space between my crisscrossed legs. Our heads side by side, he lets me hug him. I hold on.

I wonder: Who did Leo lose?

Trees can't run. Why didn't Mama and Pop? Run?

Did I?

TRAINING

Getting Ready

City kids in training. I like it. Can't keep from smiling.

Every day we hike—three, five miles, sometimes ten on Saturdays.

We hike farther, faster. Fewer breaks. More silence. More listening to birds, the scampering of hidden animals, and inhaling clean air. There's pride in how our bodies work, trekking, efficient and quick. Legs strong, shoulders back, our bodies carrying more and more weight.

We're pulling far, far…farther away from being our old selves, just city kids.

I'm becoming new. More me.

Rope School

Jamie and Dylan lead us to a glade north of camp. Ropes run across the glade, some low, some high, unstable bridges between trees, a crazy web, higher still.

Gear waits for us on picnic tables—helmets, harnesses, and ropes.

"Not climbing those," exclaims DeShon. "No way."

"Sure you are. We'll start with the low ropes, then the catwalk, then we do the high ropes, and we end with everyone's favorite, the zip line," says Dylan.

Excited, my heart pounds. There're ropes as high as eagles' nests in trees. Amazing. Can we really go up there? What if we fall?

As if I had asked, Jamie says, "It's okay, you'll be safe. You'll be in a harness, tethered the whole time."

I see—it's a maze in the sky. Dozens of white, crisscrossing ropes in the air, layered on top of each other, seeming to float.

I look for entrances, exits. There're stairs, ladders leading up several towering trees. Starting lines. High up, across the glade, are platforms, nearly hidden by branches and leaves. Finish lines.

Jamie helps us gear up—harnesses on our hips and legs. Dylan teaches us how to clip, tether ourselves to the harness and wire cable. If we fall, the cable will catch us.

"When you're climbing a mountain, you use a belay line to keep safe." Dylan attaches a rope to his harness and starts climbing.

Below him, Jamie has the rope tethered, wrapped around her waist. In seconds, Dylan is high enough that if he falls, he'll be hurt. Maybe die.

Dylan slips.

Nessa shrieks.

Jamie's arms, body weight, snaps the rope tight.

Dylan grabs a branch, wraps his arm around the trunk. "Just faking."

"Not cool," Jay scolds.

"To get down, I rappel." Dylan's knees push off—he flies backward, then swings forward, his hands grasping the rope lower. He kicks back, lowers his grip, over and over, until he's on the ground, smug, cocky.

He tries to high-five Jamie.

She ignores him, coiling the rope. "Belay or rappel," she tells us, "make sure your partner has gloves."

"I want to try," hollers Jay. Like Spider-Man, he puts all his energy into his arms, shoulders, legs.

Borrowing Jamie's gloves, I hold the belay line—letting out slack as Jay rises, ready to snap it back if his legs slip or his grip fails.

The rope is double-wrapped around my waist, my body balanced and braced.

A'Leia complains, "I'm not strong enough to hold anybody. Especially DeShon. He's huge."

"Sure you can. Belay correctly, you could hold a bear," answers Dylan. "It's all about pulleys and technique."

"Dunno," quips Kelvin. "Maybe DeShon weighs more than your average bear."

Everyone laughs, but DeShon's annoyed.

Low Ropes

"Who's next?" asks Jamie.

"Me," shouts Kelvin.

Ten feet above ground, there's a rope bridge stretching upward from one platform to another, higher platform, across the glade. The trick is to hold the rope on your left and right while stepping over gaps onto wooden slats.

Jamie checks Kelvin's tether is attached to the safety cable.

Kelvin is a wizard, practically running across the bridge like it's nothing. He doesn't once look down.

DeShon clutches the ropes, almost tiptoeing from board to board. Halfway across, he slips. The tether catches him. Through the slats, his legs dangle in the air. No one laughs.

"Come on, DeShon, you can do it," calls Kelvin.

It's my turn. I step onto the bridge. It moves, feeling elastic as I move step by step. Strange, the bridge swings not only forward and back, but also side to side. Clutching the ropes, I start to feel the rope's rhythm. With each step, the motion feels almost circular. I relax my body, flowing with the movement.

Catwalk

"Okay, that was the warm-up," says Jamie. "This will be harder. You need balance."

We're twenty feet up now. A huge log, with no ropes to hold on to, stretches between trees. If you fall, your hook and cable are the only salvation.

"It's like a balance beam," says Nessa. "I'm good on balance beams."

"I believe you," says Jay. "But a gymnastics beam is only three feet off the ground."

"I'm safe." Nessa flashes a huge smile. Then, better than a cat, she dances across.

My turn. I spread my arms to balance. It's not that hard, if you look straight ahead. Look down and it's terrifying.

Jay slips from the catwalk. Mad, he has to pull himself up onto the log. Afterward, he refuses to look at anyone. So I poke and tickle him. Laugh when he grins.

High Ropes

Nearest to us on the ground, there's a tree with a ladder. I crane my neck to see the platform at the top. Here we need to belay. A rope runs up to the platform, around a pulley, and back down. One end of the rope attaches to the harness, and one of us tethers, holding the other.

I belay for Jay as he climbs; Jamie makes sure I do it right.

Halfway up, Jay slips. The rope goes suddenly

tight around my waist and I clamp tight with my gloved hand—it doesn't take much strength. But it's a big responsibility.

"Good job," says Jamie.

Jay gives me a thumbs-up.

I'm proud, happy.

Once we've all climbed the platform, rope webbing spans the sky like a huge spiderweb. We must be a hundred feet above ground.

"Climb across," Dylan dares.

I look across the glade—at the hills beyond the camp, the tops of evergreens rolling into the horizon. A breeze stirs the treetops. I expect to see eagles but don't catch sight of any. Maybe we're the eagles now?

Jay and Kelvin crawl across like spiders. Then A'Leia and Nessa, less smooth, but still proud, cross.

"You're next, DeShon," says Dylan.

Breathing shallow, quick, DeShon leans against the tree. He won't move.

"Come on, DeShon," urges Dylan. "It's easier than the catwalk."

(*But the catwalk wasn't this high*, I think.)

DeShon doesn't speak.

"Hey," I say. "Maybe we need a water break?" Dylan looks annoyed, but I hand water to DeShon.

"Did you bring your headphones?"

"Nah."

"If you had them, what would you listen to?"

DeShon thinks, bites his lip. " 'Old Town Road,' definitely."

"You serious?"

DeShon nods.

"That's all you need. Play it in your head."

He closes his eyes, his body bouncing, his head bobbing in time to the music running in his head. His breathing slows.

"Come on," I say.

DeShon stands, tethers himself, and crawls

slowly onto and across the webbing. When he makes it to the platform, his head still bobs. He mouths: *"Can't nobody tell me nothin'...."*

Zip Line

The last platform, the final exit from the maze. A cable stretches down far beyond the glade, through the trees and into shadow. The zip line doesn't take any skill or work—you just clip and soar.

"Okay, okay, okay," says A'Leia, standing on the platform. "I'm going, I'm going."

Except she's not going. She's stuck. Fear won't let her move.

"You can do it," encourages Kelvin.

Jay winks at me. Teamwork. We've all got to be successful.

"Follow me, A'Leia." Already in my safety harness, I step in front of her. I click the metal bolt to the link on my chest. Jamie double-checks the locks while Dylan checks A'Leia's gear.

I don't know why I'm not scared. It's exciting, high in the air. I turn, squeeze A'Leia's hand.

Then, arms wide, I step off the platform.

I'm flying, my body light, sweeping through air. Looking down, I see crevices. I'm unafraid. I won't fall. I'm flying like an eagle.

Breathless, I get to the other side.

"Come on, A'Leia," I yell.

Tentative, A'Leia steps off and zooms, screaming, "I'm going to die."

My arms grab her, unhooking her from the zip line. She bursts into tears.

"It's okay, A'Leia."

Sniffling, she nods.

A'Leia, beyond scared, followed me. An ache starts in my stomach. I'm not sure why, but I'm uneasy.

"I miss Monty," she whimpers.

"Who?" I guess—Monty must be the boyfriend. "You can't go home, A'Leia. We need you. Kelvin will miss you."

"Okay." A'Leia wipes her eyes. "I'm not like

you, Addy. Not at all." Worn out, she climbs down the tree rope, collapsing on the firm ground.

One after the other, Jay, Kelvin, DeShon, and Nessa zip through the air.

Jay and I are the only ones who want to do it again. And again. I'd do it every day, all day, if I could.

Gliding, I love how bracing wind flows over my body and face.

Bibi always told me I could fly.

II

Sparks fly, dotting the carpet. Flames burst. Mama screams. I scream.

I squeeze my eyes tight. If I don't see fire, maybe it'll disappear. (Searing, suffocating heat draws close.)

Pop collapses. He screams, growls. Mama pats his flames with a dish towel, her hands. Pop writhes, twists, and turns. He won't stay still.

Mama turns. I don't recognize her face.

Glaring, she strides through the smoky room. Fire rising from a pan on the stove, licking the ceiling and walls. Fire blanketing Pop.

Arms lift me. Maya slips out of her blanket, falling, like Pop, onto the floor.

"Mama!" *I yell, yearning, trying to escape her grasp. Trying to rescue Maya.*

Pop is quiet, no longer moving.

"Fly, Adaugo," *Mama whispers. The window is open.*

Mama stops, her knees bent; she coils inward, holding, hugging me close.

Release.

I scream.

Shaken, I dress, leave the cabin. I'm used to dreaming the first dream—*when the fire starts*—over and over. *Flames reach, stretch higher and higher. Curling smoke nearly suffocates me.* I never dreamed Mama picking me up, telling me to fly.

What does it mean that I'm dreaming it now in Paradise? It doesn't make sense. A forest has no connection to a city. A cabin is way different than a tenement building.

In my heart, I know there's another dream. A dream that finishes the story. What happened to me? Did Mama let go?

I mourn Maya. It was my fault I lost her. I didn't hold her tight enough.

How did I survive and Pop and Mama die?

Awake, I still feel Mama's embrace. All the cabins are dark. In the main house there's a single light— Leo's office.

I search for sweet Ryder. He's nowhere to be found. It's too early—maybe thirty minutes until the faintest daylight shines. I grab a lantern from the porch, walk to the pasture gate. Underneath a shed, horses, Blaze and Callie, sleep. Funny how they do it standing up.

On the fence, I rest my chin on my crossed arms. I didn't know the color green had so many smells.

"Hey, Addy."

I spin around. "Jay, you scared me."

"Sorry. Don't sleep well. Noticed you're up early. Nearly every day."

"You've been spying on me?"

"No. But I know you usually meet Ryder. And Leo. This morning you're alone."

"I had a dream."

Jay leans against the fence beside me. "Dreams are bad."

"You think so?"

"I know so."

"What do you dream?"

"My younger brother getting shot."

"You saw?"

"Yeah."

I flush, feeling such sorrow. A death is a death.

"It was a drive-by. Bullet ricocheted. Benny was on the stoop, waiting for me to come home." Jay kicks the ground. "I should've been home sooner. Mama works. I'm supposed to watch him after school."

I want to tell Jay it isn't his fault. Just like it's not my fault my parents are dead. Instead, I say:

"Ryder and Leo have been teaching me how to map."

"I thought you knew how to do that."

"I mean mapping here, the forest surrounding the ranch. It's complicated. You want to come, too?"

Jay pours out the kibble. I fry the egg.

"Jay, can you grab me a coffee? Black," says Leo as if it's the most natural thing. He heads back into his office.

We follow.

Leo has already added an extra chair.

"Wow, this is cool," breathes Jay, awed by the computer's map of bright colors, straight and curved lines.

"This is where we're going to explore today." Leo points to a tiny, cursor-marked red square. "Two square miles of hillside before it becomes valley.

"Sunday, we'll start early. Explore, map the

land, the drying effects of climate change. Should be gone all day."

I watch Jay. His face is smooth, unreadable. He talks with his eyes. I don't know how he does it. But it's like his brown eyes speak a special sign language. Amazingly, I understand.

His eyes sparkle. He winks.

(Jay's going to join us!)

He smiles big, bigger, showing his dimples.

I stoop, stroke Ryder, hiding my happiness. There's a Wilderness Adventures team—then a smaller team. Us.

Me, Jay, Leo, and Ryder.

III

Saturday. Only a few weeks left of Wilderness Adventures. Then home to the city. This trip is way too short. So much for me to learn.

As soon as I get home, I know I'll want to be here. In California. On the ranch. Mapping the wild.

This morning, me, Jay, and Leo took an early hike. (Just for fun.) We let Ryder guide us, following him as he ran, stopped, sniffed, then ran some more. We didn't get lost. Didn't do anything except enjoy the wild.

Returning, the others wave, go back to writing

letters home, relaxing, hanging out. (Nobody minds we've been gone.)

Ryder, panting, tongue lolling, laps water.

Me and Jay, good tired, head straight to the rockers on the main porch. Below us, on the steps, Kelvin and A'Leia chatter about 76ers basketball.

"Doc Rivers is going to be great. Right?"

"Right," agrees A'Leia.

"I'm going to be a sports anchor."

"You can call Monty's plays."

"MON-TEE, NUMBER EIGHTY-TWO. SCORING TWENTY POINTS...TWO ON REBOUND... THE REST THREE-POINTERS...ALL-STAR MONTY WILLIAMS!!!"

A'Leia claps, cheers: "DRIBBLE IT—DRIBBLE IT—SHOOT—SHOOT—SHOOT!! TAKE THAT BALL TO THE HOOP—HOOP—HOOP!!!"

Eyebrows raised, Jay shakes his head. (As in, *These folks are crazy.*)

Even though California's superhot, A'Leia's always wearing shorts, a T-shirt, with Monty's jacket tied around her waist.

"We're going to meet up when we're back home, right?" Kelvin asks.

"Right," A'Leia answers. "You'll like Monty. He'll like you."

"Dope. You know it, right?" Then he stands. "Watch me ride Blaze?"

Goofy, Jay mouths, "Right."

A'Leia still doesn't like to ride. (Nobody else does, either.) But wherever Kelvin goes, she goes. Me and Jay watch her rooting for Kelvin as Blaze trots around the pen.

"Press your legs into Blaze's sides." (Jamie is the official riding instructor.) "You're trotting. Now see if you can get Blaze to canter."

A'Leia covers her eyes, squealing.

"Click your tongue," shouts Jamie. "Back straight. Head up."

Kelvin and Blaze are moving—*ba-ba-dum, ba-ba-dum, ba-ba-dum*.

"Go, Kelvin," screams Jay.

I jump up. "Go!"

"Rein her in. *Slow, slow.*"

Kelvin tightens the reins. Blaze slows to a trot, then a walk. Wearing the wildest smile, Kelvin pushes his eyeglasses high on his nose. Across the field, happy A'Leia does the same.

Me and Jay laugh.

Midday, Leo sets a serving table on the porch. "Outdoors lunch."

I set paper plates, forks. Sweating, Leo lifts chicken off the outdoor grill. Using pot holders, Jay carries a huge pot of potatoes from the kitchen. Dylan tosses the salad.

Beaming, Jamie carries the cake. "Lemon chiffon."

"You baked it?" asks Nessa.

"Absolutely. Chiffon cake was created by a California man."

"Cheesesteaks were created in Philly," adds A'Leia.

"New York's got pizza, bagels, and cheesecake. I could go on," boasts Jay. "Nathan's hot dogs. New York pastrami, corned beef, baked pretzels, New

York Italian ices, and don't forget"—he pauses, dramatic—"Manhattan clam chowder."

"And deep-fried Twinkies," I yell. (Though I never ate one.)

Nessa rolls her eyes. "Jersey's got saltwater taffy and hoagies. Perfect for the Jersey Shore."

"Nothing beats the Pacific Ocean," Dylan states flatly. "Or California food."

For the first time, Leo grimaces.

I expect him to say "Wilderness is best. Nothing beats cooking over an open fire."

Instead, he says, "There's no place like home."

"Dorothy!" squeals Nessa like she's on a game show.

Leo smiles. "But I think Dorothy made a mistake. Home can be anywhere. Even Oz. Landscapes call to all of us. What's the point of journeying, mapping, if you can't find home?"

"*Feel* home," I say. Everyone quiets, staring at me. Embarrassed, I bounce down the steps, walk closer to the forest, and sit beneath a tree.

"Want this, Addy?" Jay hands me my backpack. (How'd he know?)

I set my plate on the ground. (Ants are going to love it.) Brows lifted, questioning, Jay points at my plate. I nod. He lifts the plate and starts eating the chicken.

Chomping, he gazes at me. I know exactly what he's thinking. *This chicken's good. My mama's is better.*

I pull out my notepad. I need to map. I twirl my pencil. I've already mapped Paradise Ranch before. I still hate there's only one driveway, one EXIT. Hate that I have to leave. (But love how I'll soon be hugging Bibi.)

I start drawing Paradise Ranch. The landscape, as it is now. Main house. Barn. Horse field. Pig trough. Then I quickly add people. Leo, Jamie, and Dylan, eating on the porch. Kelvin and A'Leia, on the steps, their heads close together, stuffing themselves with cake.

DeShon's on a blanket, with a book, underneath an oak tree.

"Snakes," he announces. "Aka reptiles. Just

like lizards, turtles, crocodiles." His finger moves across the page.

"What're you tracing?" asks Jay.

"A California king. It's black with white and yellow bands. Know why it's called king? It eats other snakes. Especially rattlers.

"Wish we had more snakes in the city," he says, wistful. "Leo says global warming will make it harder for them to shed their skin or have babies. Too much heat, they'll die."

I sketch me and Jay, two feet south of DeShon. Behind us, the never-ending forest stands watch.

Where's Nessa?

I see her wearing DeShon's headphones, dancing for the chickens. Like a smooth marionette, she's swishing her arms, kicking her legs. Next she does the Whoa—bouncing and locking, then a little bit of the Toosie slide. Sadie, Penny, and Marigold are clucking, their tiny wings fluttering as they step lively in the coop.

Last night, before bed, Nessa told me she was

going to try out for dance crew in the fall. "Better than a cheerleader," she said, but I wouldn't know.

I draw lines—long, short, broken lines. I'm drawing a maze. Making paths for Nessa, DeShon, Kelvin, and A'Leia to find me.

Next to me, Jay swallows a spoonful of mashed potatoes.

On paper, I draw a line between us. Then another line, sharp to the right, then left, then another sharp right. Not too complicated.

Strange. I've drawn a beginner's maze. I'm the goal—the used-to-be outsider waiting to be found.

I'm going to miss Paradise Ranch. Miss Nessa, Jay, A'Leia, Kelvin, and DeShon.

IV

Sunday morning, a long hike. Me and Jay trek alongside Leo. We're exploring one square mile at a time in the northwest. There're still thousands of miles left to explore. Google Maps details the acres. But for me, the best joy is feeling, trudging, measuring the land myself. My sketchpad is nearly full.

It's early. The air is still crisp.

Ryder runs everywhere, disappearing among trees, only coming back to us when Leo whistles.

Off the trails, we surprise animals—a gray fox, black-tailed deer. Some animals we identify by footprints—black bears, bobcats—and some by what they've left, snake skins or deer poop. At the stream, we find dozens of raccoon footprints.

"Raccoons wash all their food," says Leo. "Better than most people."

"No way!" exclaims Jay.

"Yes way," says Leo, grinning.

I like looking up, discovering eagles' nests wedged between branches. They're huge, four to five feet in diameter, two to four feet deep.

"Grass, feathers, and twigs," says Leo, "make for a soft center."

The ridge above us is heavy, dense with trees. There're at least three nests. I imagine climbing towering trees, spying on eggs and eaglets.

"Let's draw here." Me and Leo share a box of colored pencils. I like how we both draw the same area, then compare. "Later, we'll make a definitive set, Addy. We can mail back and forth."

California to New York. New York to California.

*　*　*

I'm too overwhelmed to say anything. As if knowing something important happened, Jay stops throwing a stick for Ryder. He looks back as if to ask, "You okay?"

I smile.

Jay nods. Throws the stick into the stream. Ryder jumps, *splash*, into the water.

The ranch is great. But I think this moment is paradise. Surrounded by nature—a gurgling stream, the caws, chirps of birds, a forest quiet humming underneath all the other sounds. Me, drawing maps. Leo, my teacher. And Jay playing fetch with Ryder.

I keep drawing, losing track of time.

"Hey, Ryder. Ryder!" It's Jay.

I look up, catching Ryder rushing between trees, disappearing north.

He barks. It's a wild bark, a warning. More ferocious than I've ever heard before.

The wind shifts. I pause, lifting my chin. I smell—what? A hint of smoke?

Leo whistles. "Ryder, what is it, boy?"

We wait. Ryder doesn't come running; he keeps barking.

"Smoke," I say, frowning. "I'm sure of it."

Leo's expression clouds. "Let's go."

We're running toward the sound. After a few minutes, Ryder is in front of us. Trying to lead us. Barking, lifting his paws excitedly, then dashing away from us.

A campground with a pit.

"Campers?" I ask Leo.

He nods.

"Messy," says Jay, picking up candy wrappers.

Leo squats. Lifts a cigarette stub. Several have been smashed in the dirt.

I frown. Smoking is horrible. Mr. Greaves, the deacon at church, died of lung cancer. But fire smoke is worse, reminding me of dreams and death.

Barking, sharp, short, it's like Ryder's saying, *Here. Here. See. See.*

Leo steps gingerly toward the shallow pit. He squats, his open palm above the ashes, burnt and unburnt bark. "It's still warm."

Me and Jay move closer, squatting, too.

"Inexperienced campers. Or else lazy, thoughtless."

"It'll die out, won't it?" asks Jay.

Sad-eyed, Leo looks at both of us. "A breeze could lift a spark, start a blaze. It wouldn't take much. There hasn't been enough rain."

Panicked, I look at the towering trees, the brown undergrowth. Fire. I can't imagine it. But there's a reason trees are chopped into firewood. I squeeze my eyes tight. I don't want to imagine.

Leo murmurs, *"Some say the world will end in fire / Some say in ice . . . / I hold with those who favor fire.*

"Robert Frost. A poet. He must've foreseen global warming." Leo shakes like he's inside a bad dream.

I step closer. I want to comfort Leo. (We both distrust fire.)

"Jay, Addy, hiking off-trail, camping overnight,

exploring wilderness, you might need a fire to eat, keep away animals, stay warm. But don't you ever forget," Leo says fiercely, "how to put it out."

"You drown it with water. Mix ashes and embers, making sure they're all wet."

"That didn't happen here."

"Right, Jay."

"What if you don't have water?" I ask.

"Dirt will do. It'll smother a dying flame."

Jay holds his hand above the pit. "I can still feel heat." He pours water from his canteen.

"That's right. Use your hands if you have to. Touch. Make sure there's no warmth."

"I'm going to add dirt. Just to make sure." I scoop handfuls and handfuls of dirt.

"Double-check again."

I push my hand into the soot and dirt. "It's out."

Jay pulls his bandana from his pocket. "Use this, Addy."

I clean my trembling hand. Anxiety grips me. Like a flash, I see fire everywhere.

Rapidly, I blink back tears as Leo speaks.

* * *

"Forests burn. Animals' homes are destroyed. As our planet warms, there are more heat-related deaths."

Leo stares far off into the forest. He looks tired, worn, older. This scares me, too.

He turns abruptly, hiking back the way we came.

Surprised, me and Jay both lift our brows. No more exploring topography, nature.

If this were a maze, I think, the fire pit would be the END. The uncovered surprise. But instead of treasure, we averted disaster.

V

Graduation. Our final adventure. Four days of hiking, three nights of overnight camping. DeShon groans. (Not too much.) Everyone else is happy. I'm thrilled.

Jamie surprises us with s'mores. "Can't leave Wilderness Adventures without having some more s'mores."

We groan.

"This is white people's food," jokes Kelvin.

Us kids laugh. It's kinda true. Before this summer, none of us had ever had s'mores.

*   *   *

No city kid toasts marshmallows on a stick. Let alone over an outdoor fire.

The white, fluffy sugar pillows blaze. If it catches fire, you have to blow it out before it's burnt. (Nessa's marshmallows keep catching fire, burning black.)

"Why put a perfectly soft, sweet, warm marshmallow between graham crackers? I don't get it," says DeShon, munching as he toasts three marshmallows at a time.

"It's the chocolate, DeShon," answers Jay, licking his fingers. "Warm marshmallows make the chocolate ooze."

Kelvin puts his finger to his lips. *Don't tell*, he's signaling. (Especially Jamie.)

Kelvin steals the chocolate squares. Over and over, he toasts marshmallows, mashes them between crackers. But he doesn't eat them. Just the chocolate.

I don't toast s'mores. Too close to the fire.

Jay makes me s'mores. He's a really good guy. I probably never would've met him in New York. Wouldn't have known a guy could be a good friend. That Jay could know me without me saying a word.

I think s'mores are pretty good.

Jamie and Dylan pour a bucket of water on the fire. They stir until it seems all the wood, coals, and twigs are wet.

"Wait," shouts Jay as we turn toward our cabins. "You gotta double-check. Make sure it's really out."

"You're an expert now?" Dylan asks, sarcastic.

"He is since I taught him," Leo boasts.

Dylan abruptly turns, heading toward his cabin.

(Leo winks. He knows I know Dylan isn't the best counselor.)

Jay's palm moves over the pit. "Cool," he says. Then he stuffs his hand deep in the wet ash. "Really cool," he says, looking up at me.

We understand. The fire is out.

TRAPPED

Overnight Camp

Eagle's Ridge is gorgeous. I don't tell anyone I saw it from The Lookout. It's me and Leo's secret. And Ryder's. And the eagle's, too.

Seeing the bird fly, I know it's the same eagle I saw with Leo.

This is the best day ever. Hiking with packs full of tents, water, food is much harder. Three weeks ago we never would've made it. This time no one complained. Not even DeShon.

We finish securing our orange tents. Jamie and A'Leia share a tent. Nessa's with me; Jay's with

DeShon; Kelvin and Dylan share the last tent. Nature is our toilet (we dug a deep, narrow hole). When we leave, we'll stuff it with leaves, dirt.

Jay's built a fire. I don't like it; everybody else loves it.

I check my backpack. Flashlight. A knife, rope, PowerBars, water bottle, compass, first aid kit, a topographical map, my sketchpad, a hardcover novel, and a book Leo gave me on topography.

"A bit overprepared, aren't you, Addy?" Dylan grins, but I can tell he thinks I'm funny. (Not in a good way.)

I turn my back on him.

Leo's taking care of the ranch animals. If he were here, he'd say, "No such thing as overprepared."

Dylan and Jamie are nice, but they're just college kids. Leo is the real deal—a wilderness man. He's teaching me.

A gust of air touches my cheek.

I lift my head, snatching a whiff of some new smell. Not dark green or light green. Not the musk of forest animals. Or decomposing leaves, fallen branches. Not even the smell of Jay's fire.

Foreboding grips me. Something's not right.

Walking to the ridge's edge, I stare down into deep darkness. I know there's water below, twisting through the valley. It's a narrow pass. Forested hills, then mountains, on either side.

The stars don't provide enough light to see clearly. But my mind sees what my eyes can't. It's almost as if I can *feel* the land, feel the geography.

Another wind burst.

"Bibi?"

I hear: *"You're always journeying whether you like it or not."* I'm not sure if it's memory or if I really *do* hear Bibi's voice.

I squat, letting my fingers brush at the dirt, the solid rock.

Bibi must've hated crossing the Atlantic. I wonder if she'd like living here? In the western wilderness? Or we could go to Nigeria. They have eagles. Peaks. Mountain ridges.

I feel—something. *Fear?* Something, someone stalking?

I'm anxious. Maybe I'm just imagining?

My summer adventure is going to end. I'm sad. I don't want it to end.

"Lights out," calls Jamie.

"Never thought I'd be in a sleeping bag on the ground," chortles Kelvin. A'Leia pokes him. "Stop." He sticks out his tongue.

But us city kids get it. Never knew we'd end up liking hiking and camping. Even DeShon sometimes leaves off his headphones to listen to birds, breezes rumbling through the trees.

No one fusses about bedtime.

"I want to watch the fire," says Jay. "Make sure it's out."

Dylan nods. "Suit yourself. Don't be too long."

* * *

The sleeping bags are lightweight; the summer evenings still get cold. So everyone will sleep in their clothes.

Kelvin and Dylan have already turned off their lantern. Jamie and A'Leia are making hand shadows on the tent wall. I suspect DeShon is "lights out," though I bet his music is on. Bass streaming softly into his ears.

"Coming, Addy?"

"In a sec, Nessa."

She giggles. I don't care if she thinks me and Jay are a couple. We *are* friends. I'm going to miss him.

"We'll stay friends?" asks Jay, poking embers with his stick. "Leo said I could come back."

"You read my mind. Friends. Hope I see you in New York, too."

Grinning, he lifts his head.

An owl calls. *Whooo, whoooooo.* A gust of wind

rustles, scratches pine needles, oak leaves. I plop, sit beside him on the log, watching the dying fire.

Jay is strong, kind, a good partner and team player. But he's not looking at me. He's looking at ashes, gray coals, and blackened soot and bark.

Sad. I feel his sadness. He's like me—not wanting to leave. Wanting and not wanting to return home.

"I wish Grandma Bibi were here. Eleven years she's been in the city. She'd love the forest. She'd like Leo."

"I wish my little brother could've seen this."

"I've got a good book. *Hatchet*. Leo gave it to me. Want to borrow it?"

Jay looks directly at me. "You trying to make me feel better?"

"Yeah, I am."

Jay grins. "Leo gave me a book, too. *My Side of the Mountain*. A New York city kid runs away to the woods."

"In *Hatchet*, the kid survives a plane crash in the wilderness. At least that's what Leo says. I haven't started it yet."

* * *

Jamie and Dylan (and Kelvin and A'Leia) must be asleep. I remember asking Jamie—"In an emergency. Are you responsible for us in an emergency?"

She didn't have a plan.

"I have to have the plan," I blurt, without realizing it.

"You always have a plan, Addy. The rest of us just hike. You're always watching, looking for paths, trails. Isn't that what a map is? Entrances, exits? Isn't that what you did on the plane?" Jay grins. "If the plane fell, I wouldn't have been surprised if you grew wings."

"Funny," I say. But I feel good inside. Suddenly, shy.

To be triple safe, Jay adds more water, then shovels more dirt. He holds his palm above the pit, then plunges his hands into the dirt. It's a bit scary— what if the flames aren't all died down?

But Jay knows his job. He lifts his hands, covered with sticky dirt, soot, and ash. He's happy; I'm happy. Cool Jay, acting like a kid, with mud pies.

*   *   *

We hear a tremoring, a rush of flapping wings. Then a shriek.

Danger. I'm reminded of screams in my dreams. *Danger.*

"Owl found his dinner." Jay rinses his hands, heads toward his tent. "Night, Addy."

I'm uneasy. Scared of what?—I don't know. My hands shake.

I stare into the midnight forest, with its dark, towering shapes. There's life inside it.

In trees, along the ridge, eagles (my eagle) are sleeping. I should be sleeping. We're safe. I have my maps. I have my friends.

Then, inside my mind, I hear whispering: *I have me.*

II

I'm twisting, turning, restless in my sleeping bag. When I feel I'm falling into dreaming, I jolt myself awake. *I'm not going to dream.*

Nessa is sleeping hard. She's coiled inside her sleeping bag like a baby bear.

I smell smoke. We're not in our cabin with a dying fire. *Smoke?*

I'm not dreaming of Pop, dying in a kitchen fire, or Mama lifting me up, to save me.

Smoke floats. Into the tent. My nose. My eyes.

I jolt awake. I slip on my shoes, grab my backpack. "Be prepared. Always," Leo taught me. Up and out.

Outside the tent, the acrid smell is stronger. Jay's fire is dead. I look north, south, east, then west. Through the forest, lining the mountain range, I see layers of color: orange, yellow, red, topped by gray smoke. Fire.

"Fire!" I scream. I lift the tent's flap. "Nessa, get up. Fire!"

I rush to each of the tents, yelling. Everyone's confused, groggy.

But not Jay. Alert, he moves, shaking DeShon. "Get up, man."

Jamie wakes, blinking like I'm crazy. "What're you talking about?"

Dylan rushes out, staring west. He curses.

Soon everyone is outside screaming, yelling. The mountain range behind us is aglow. There are popping bursts like gunshots or fireworks.

"Dry trees," says Jamie, awed. "I've read this. They explode, spread sparks."

"New fires," adds Jay, emphatic.

Pop, pop, pop. Dozens of new fires, starkly lit, against the darkened sky.

Nessa, crying, grips my hand.

We're all awestruck—watching the flames reach higher into the sky, creating snakelike trails. Fire across the ridge, down the mountainside, spreading inland, tree by tree, burning like massive candles, *pop-pop-popp*ing and falling, striking more trees, burning ground cover, eating the landscape alive.

"We've got to get out of here," I shout.

"Where?" asks Kelvin.

"Grab your packs," Jamie screams. *She's going to keep us safe,* I think. Then she and Dylan start arguing. *Which way? Which way?*

Dylan is trying, over and over, to call on his cell even though he knows there's no signal.

Jamie pales. Dylan paces, cursing louder and louder.

Wind speed picks up, blowing east. Unnaturally warm air breezes past me.

Time slows. I look—the fire is making a maze. Zigzagging, moving in straight, then diagonal lines. Inside my head, I *see* it.

If Eagle's Ridge is the END, I ought to be able to figure a way back to Paradise Ranch. To Leo and Ryder.

But I didn't draw this maze. Worse, the drawing—the burning, destroying—isn't done. A gobbling, eating-the-air fire isn't imaginary. It isn't a dream. It's creating its own wild patterns, disrupting, destroying paths.

A dead end in this maze really will be a dead end.

In daylight, without the fire, it took a long, hard hike to get to Eagle's Ridge. In darkness, with the fire, it'd be beyond hard.

I'm so scared, I want to scream.

Nessa is whimpering. "Hold on," I say.

"Let's head to the ranch," says DeShon.

"Can't," I say. "The ranch is north. The fire is sweeping up the whole ridge. We'll be trapped."

"It's worth a try," insists Jamie.

I try solving the maze in my head.

We're all standing, petrified, watching the fire roar and advance.

A'Leia coughs. Then Kelvin. Gusts of smoke overwhelm us.

I look for a way out. I hear my pop's scream. I push it away. *Focus*. Then I see it.

"Down the cliff," I urge. "We've got to climb down, south, then turn east. It's the only way."

"Are you crazy?" asks Jamie. "The ranch is north."

Dylan curses again, adding, "You're crazy, Addy. Fire's to the west. Spreading northeast."

"But it will stall. Stay north of the cliff at least for a while. Please, listen to me!"

"We should head north. Hilly, mountainous. But it's the only way," says Dylan.

"And what if the fire moves faster than we can hike? We'd be climbing right into the fire. Not smart. Our only escape would be to outrun the fire."

"I'm in charge." Angrily, Dylan pushes himself close.

I stand tall. I won't back down. I try reason: "You're forgetting wind, Dylan. Look, the smoke is shifting, getting darker."

"You don't know everything, Addy."

I cringe. How to explain Leo's taught me a lot? Or how maps are a second language for me?

How to explain sometimes (not always) I sense patterns even before they're made?

"Listen," I scream. "Going down the cliff, we'll reach water. An escape. A way out."

"If we don't fall or die first," Dylan sneers.

"We've got to go. We'll make it."

"So, you know everything?"

Jamie's no longer the bubbly college girl. She's scowling, scared.

"I know the map." *I see it.*

"Look." Nessa points upward.

Birds that should be sleeping are flying northward in flocks. Specks rushing hurriedly through the hazy sky.

Kelvin coughs, doubling over, gasping, "Can't—breathe."

"Asthma," says A'Leia.

Dumbfounded, we stare.

Steadying Kelvin, she stutters, "He won't carry

his inhaler. I warned him. 'Air's clean. Clear,' he kept saying."

Dumb, dumb. Dumb.

"He thought he didn't need it," whimpers A'Leia.

"He didn't tell us." Jamie's stricken.

I feel sorry for her.

"If I'd known, I'd have carried a spare."

A blanket of smoke quickly floats downward.

"Kelvin," screams A'Leia.

Kelvin's coughing so hard, tears stream from his eyes.

Roar. From the south. Another roar. A raging fire has a sound. *I remember it.* A gravelly, continuous exhale. Like Darth Vader breathing, threatening.

"It's closer. Getting closer," cries Nessa.

Fire races. Quick, powerful puffs of wind create brush and bush sparks, trees become mammoth flaming candles. Every branch a wick. *Roar...roar.*

Then no roaring. Crackling, snapping, burning.

Whoosh—air's being sucked out of the universe, making a vacuum.

I tremble. *I remember this.* Fire's alive, a thickening, ravenous monster. Quieter, it appears to pause, retreat. Then it roars, more explosive than ever, and leaps.

There. At the camp's edges. And there. There.

Flames have skipped closer to us. Taunting, tantalizing.

Jamie, Dylan, and the others stumble back behind the dead campfire.

"We go south. Now. Grab your packs," I shriek. "Shoes." Smoke seeps into our eyes, mouth, hair. I smell it on my clothes. But it's the heat that's most unsettling. Hot—too, too hot. *Like the frying oil exploding in the pan on the stove.*

"Back to the ranch," orders Dylan, taking charge.

"What if we don't make it?" yells Jay.

"We have to," Jamie answers. "Kelvin needs his inhaler."

A'Leia and Jamie half walk, half drag Kelvin.

They follow Dylan. "Come on with me. All of you."

Jay, DeShon, Nessa don't move.

I'm shocked.

Crack.

Falling wood hits DeShon's and Jay's tent. Flames race, searing orange nylon. Jay dashes, drags his pack out. Blackened fabric curls, spreads.

Nessa grips my hand. "I'm following you."

DeShon snaps, "Which way, Addy?"

They're counting on me.

Fire's coming. *Like it came for me when I was little.* Wind blows, steady, relentless. Fire will swallow the forest, our camp.

Dylan's stopped. Waiting for us. "Come on," he yells, desperate.

I'm wavering, ready to break down. Nessa's, Jay's, and DeShon's lives matter.

Bam. Whoosh.

A tall tree cracks, branches burst, and the trunk falls.

"Jump back," yells Jay.

Flames scatter crazily, lighting the brush, swiftly sweeping up several other trees. Wind gusts.

"It's surrounding us." A'Leia's panicked.

Jay starts to dart ahead. I grab his arm, shaking my head.

Fire's made a barrier—split us into groups.

"You won't make it, Jay. You'll be set afire."

His body slumps. His eyes mirror his pain.

Heat is intense. Not just the flames but the smoke. We're too close. Our airways are irritated, inflamed.

I hear Dylan urging, "Cover your mouth, cover your mouth. Smoke kills first."

I pull my shirt up over my mouth and nose.

I look behind us. Only twisted metal remains of the tents. Fire crawls, cutting off another path.

"Nessa!" Jamie hollers. "DeShon."

Through the flames, Jamie looks like a mirage. A shaky illusion. She's too close, too close to the booming fire, trying to break through.

Dylan holds her back. He yells, "Kelvin, A'Leia, keep going. Hurry. We'll be right behind you."

Jamie's crying. Dylan's dragging her away from the flaming barrier.

Another gust. Another tree falls. New lines, new obstacles. Flames twist, lick the air, stretching miles high. A deadly maze.

Me, Nessa, Jay, DeShon, on our own.

"Come on," I start leading them out of the blistering maze. A zigzag move. First toward fire; then down toward water.

III

We're running for our lives.

A fire can't burn if there isn't fuel. Eagle's Ridge has dry, mature trees, overgrown brush. But nearer the river, moisture. Trees there will be slower to catch.

"Hold here."

Topography, understanding the land.

Eagle's Ridge's side is craggy, uneven. It's over four hundred feet until the bottom. But there're plateaus, ledges to rest on. Better yet, if we can make it to the first ledge, there's a cascading trail. It's rough, a steep incline, but hikeable. (I saw it on one of Leo's maps.)

*   *   *

I search for the least-steep path (topography lines drawn with wide spaces between). "An almost trail," Leo said. "Over time, climbers have etched the best way down. Or up."

But, first, we've got to climb over jutting cliffs before we reach the easiest path to journey down.

"We need to get to that ledge. About forty feet down."

"Are you sure about this?" murmurs Jay.

"Yes, I see it."

Jay doesn't ask how. He simply nods.

I swing my backpack to the ground, search for my flashlight. I double-check the trail. Light trips over pebbles, rocks, dirt... searches for the fewest weeds, fallen branches, and twigs... searches for where brush has been worn away.

I'm sweating. Nighttime air is hot. Fire moves, relentless. "Here. Over here."

Stowing the light, I pull out rope, hand the loop to Jay.

His eyes widen. He gets it.

Jay tethers the rope to a boulder, then wraps it around his waist.

I slip on my backpack, turning for the last time, flinching at the horrific flames destroying our camp.

I start. Feet, hands gripping rock.

DOWN.

Rock tears my shirt. My breath's ragged.

I don't look down, way down where I know there's water. I just look at crusty rock in front of me, the faraway plateau below me.

"You're gonna die," screams Nessa.

"We're not going to make it," shouts DeShon.

Jay lets out the rope inch by inch as my feet and arms move, search for any grip, any edge. I try to rappel, kick back and swing, but I'm not very good.

Above me, Nessa and DeShon stare, open-mouthed and anxious.

Jay's eyes speak: *You can do it. You can do it, Addy.*

Calves aching, I control my body, alternating between inching and trying to rappel down.

Relieved, exhaling, I make it to the ledge.

Jay pulls up the rope.

"Next," I holler.

Jay's knotting the rope around Nessa's waist. (He's worried she won't hold on.)

"You can do it, Nessa," I shout.

Helpless, I watch as she steps off the ridge, then twists. Flails.

So she doesn't free-fall, Jay and DeShon clench the rope.

"Use your feet, hands, Nessa. Kick, climb down."

I moan. Nessa doesn't have shoes.

(DeShon? Jay? Am I the only one wearing shoes?)

The ridge is hard, rough. Nessa's not wailing anymore. She's focused. Scared, but focused. Slowly, slow, bit by bit, a foot, then another, she finds an edge; one hand, then the other, clings to rock, lowering her body.

DOWN.

"Hurry, Nessa," yells DeShon. "Fire's close."

Nessa's right leg buckles. DeShon and Jay tighten the rope. Pebbles, rocks skitter down. I cover my face.

"Come on, Nessa."

DOWN.

DOWN.

I clasp her waist. Nessa, her arms tight around my throat, nearly chokes me. "You're safe," I soothe, partly lying. Not adding the words: *For now.*

I untie the rope and it zips upward. The moon, a shimmering orange-yellowish halo, is behind Jay and DeShon.

"Hurry, DeShon."

DeShon nods at Jay, then kicks off the edge and swings a third of the way down. Jay, taut and grim-faced, anticipates when to loosen or tighten the rope.

I'm anxious. Why did Jay, Nessa, and DeShon believe in me?

I don't really know what I'm doing. I don't want the responsibility.

If I hadn't hesitated, they'd all be safe with Jamie and Dylan.

DeShon leaps, letting himself drop the last foot. He unties the rope.

Jay lets the rope drop, hollering, "Catch."

(There's no one left to hold it.) He has to rely on his strength—gaining a foothold, a grip on sharp rock. There's no safety if he falls.

The fire's advancing glow is brighter, higher than ever. (No doubt Jay feels it.)

"Come on, Jay," I whisper, relieved he's wearing hiking boots.

Me, DeShon, and Nessa, straining our necks upward, feel Jay's every move.

DOWN.

He's moving fast. Too fast. He slips; his right leg, shoulder, and arm wing backward, upsetting his balance.

DOWN.

Nessa gasps. Her hands cover her mouth.

Come on, Jay, come on repeats inside my head. *Come on.*

He rebalances. More slowly, carefully, he places his hands and feet.

He jumps onto the ledge. Me, Nessa, DeShon hug him. We hug each other. For the moment, we're safe from the raging fire above.

Safe, on a narrow mountainside plateau.

ESCAPE

I

"That was the hard part," I say encouragingly, hoping I'm right.

True, we don't need to drop down to another ridge. We need to hike an informal trail—stumble on, as quick as possible, in the dark, down a dangerous hill.

I squeeze my eyes shut.

Think, Addy. Think. See.

Now haze, smoke cloud the view. What if we get disoriented?

The path is still wild, and it'd be easy—*too easy*—for someone to slip, spin, fall down the hillside.

I squat, zip open my backpack. Compass. Leo gave it to me. I hand Jay the flashlight. He, Nessa, and DeShon are standing above me.

It's like I can read their minds: *Now what?*

Like a small miracle, the arrow quivers. I hold my hand out, moving it until the compass points due south.

"How far?" asks Jay.

I hesitate. I only plotted the escape from the fire above. Not the rest of the path. So I just say, "That way."

DeShon looks worried. Nessa bites her lip.

"You've got this, Addy," says Jay.

I smile weakly.

"Someone will rescue us," Nessa insists. "Do you think the others made it? Back to the ranch?"

Skeptical, Jay lifts his brow.

I keep quiet.

Nessa sits cross-legged beside me. "My feet hurt," she says simply.

We're sitting close together. Our hands are scratched, battered. Jay's palms are badly rope-burned. DeShon's and Nessa's socks are dirty, torn. Their feet bruised.

It feels strange to be on a narrow, mossy ledge. Fire above, water below. Two feet farther left, we'd be in danger of tumbling down.

Above us, on the ridges, trees are exploding uncontrollably.

We flinch. Nessa screams.

"Heads up. Heads up," warns Jay.

Burning tree parts—trunk, branch, leaves— fall, swirl off the ridge's edge, crashing into the valley and stream.

We huddle, our arms trying to provide cover for each other's heads.

Like snow, black and gray ash cloaks us.

"We've got to go." I gag, spit dust.

The roar above is thunderous, growling, growing closer. Wind shifts northward. There's nothing to stop sparks, burning tree limbs from flying, singeing, killing us all.

Just as we move, the fire moves, too. Snaps at our heels.

"Nessa, put on my hiking boots," I insist.

I pull out *Hatchet*. Lay out the MedKit's scissors, gauze, and tape. "Book covers can protect our feet. Better than nothing."

"Got it," says Jay, pulling *My Side of the Mountain* from his backpack. "DeShon, take my boots."

"Can't take them, man."

"We'll share."

DeShon nods.

I toss antiseptic wipes. "Wipe first, then soft gauze, then book covers. Then tape."

Me and Jay craft pathetic imitation shoes.

"I'll share, too," murmurs Nessa.

I don't say a word. Even with boots, Nessa's the slowest hiker.

Another burning tree barrels down the ridge, bouncing off the hillside, before landing. *Boom.* Smaller explosions burst red with orange flames.

I flinch.

"We need to move now," I urge, standing, off-balance. "We need to move."

DeShon grimaces, favoring his left foot.

Nessa helps Jay. Book covers aren't Air Jordans.

Close to our ledge, a burning branch bounces off rock, falls.

Frightened, Nessa starts hyperventilating. Smoke strains her lungs, deepening, quickening her gasps.

Jay wraps his arm around her. "Nothing's going to happen to you, Nessa."

"What he said," says DeShon, pretending not to be scared.

Jay watches me.

He wants me to calm Nessa. Repeat: *Nothing's going to happen to you.*

But stuff happens. Who knows who'll be hurt?

Fire has come for me twice. Parents dead. Painful dreams. I can't figure out how (or why) I'm alive.

"There's always a way out. Use your mind, your heart."

Survive.

But until now, I've only been responsible for me.

Jay's awesome; Nessa's kind; and DeShon's actually a good guy. They're my crew—never had one before. Who knew? Never knew how much I needed one.

I hug Nessa. "We're going to have pizza when we escape."

Determinedly, I step back, extend my arm, my palm down. "Survive."

Jay lays his hand on top of mine. "Survive."

DeShon grunts, smacks his hand down on our two. "Survive."

"Survive," adds Nessa, her hand quivering. "Survive."

II

I lead, following the glow-in-the-dark compass. Our thighs and knees ache from going downhill, stepping, sliding over rough terrain. We're filthy, spitting out ash, wiping it from our eyes, noses. Our hair's gray.

DeShon's ankle twists. He curses. "Sorry," he says, limping.

Not much else we can do except push on.

Wildfire won't wait.

We trudge, exhausted, hungry. We have water breaks. But I keep insisting, "Move, come on. Fire spreads fast."

Silent, we walk in line, trying to avoid falling

in the dark. Everyone's coughing, trying our best not to inhale too deep.

DeShon's and Nessa's steps thump; me and Jay scrape dirt and rock. *Thump, scrape, thump, scrape.*

"We can do it," encourages Jay.

Glum, Nessa moans.

DeShon starts singing "Old Town Road."

Nessa tries to smother a giggle.

Jay's tenor soars.

We move, walk on until stars fade, until the sun rises in the east.

Despite the smoke, seeing faint glimmers of sunlight, I'm happy. Traveling east, it seems like our omen.

My feet fly out from beneath me. My chin bounces on dirt. Blood drips.

The compass disappears, rattling over the edge into water.

No one speaks.

(So much for good omens.)

"I've got this." Jay takes my pack, flips open the MedKit. He wipes my hands, taking extra care with my chin before bandaging. "We should rest, Addy."

"Got to go."

I scan everyone's faces, trying to read them.

Nessa's biting her lip, and I guess she's been crying again. DeShon, trying to keep weight off his sprained ankle, looks at the ground instead of me.

Jay's jaw is clenched, his eyes challenging. Still, if I asked him to keep moving, I think he'd do it.

I scan the hillside; the fire is less fierce above, but we're not at the stream. We haven't fully left the wildfire's maze. Ash flakes still fall.

I exhale. We've hiked for the day, set up camp, run for our lives, and hiked all night. I want to say "Let's go on." Instead, wiping away ash from my eyes, I say,

"Let's rest. Rain ponchos are in the backpacks."

EXIT.

We've made it to safety, for now.

On the ground, huddling beneath ponchos blocking out ash, thin streaks of light, we hold on to each other and breathe. In and out; in and out. Sleep-deprived, our breath shallow and soothing, we drift in and out of sleep. A head jerks, a hand slides, someone tilts. We try our best to hold on to one another. There's still a chance one or more of us will tumble off the trail.

Together, we keep each other safe.

(Maybe it's not all on me?)

Eyelids heavy, my head droops.

"Smother it, smother it." Panicking, Mama swats with a dish towel, a frying pan of flames. Pop stomps, making more sparks. The ceiling and carpet burn.

Mama screams, "Adaugo, Adaugo! You must go. Go. Adaugo!"

I wake, screaming.

Single file. Keep moving. Feet, legs ache. Keep moving. Lungs constrict; shoulders tense; muscles contract. Keep moving.

Almost there.

Bibi's voice resonates: "To know yourself, you need to journey, Adaugo. Remember what's forgotten."

"Hey, what, who's Adaugo?" asks DeShon, bringing up the rear. "You were screaming it."

"It's me," I holler, my eyes fixed ahead.

"I thought your name was Addy," Nessa squeaks.

"Adaugo?" asks Jay, right behind me. "What's that mean?"

I'm glad I can't see his face. Glad I can't see any of them. My name marks me as different. (I'm already different.)

At least they waited, didn't embarrass me right away by letting me know I woke them with my screams.

(I'm sensitive about my name. Teachers pronounce it "A-da-ooo-go."

I have to explain, "It's African. A-dah-go." But some still can't get it right. Can't understand how alphabet letters in other countries have different sounds.)

"Fate. No deny, Adaugo. Daughter of an eagle."

"I like Adaugo better than Addy."

"Thanks, Nessa." Then I murmur, "Daughter of an eagle."

"What?" ask Jay and DeShon.

"Daughter of an eagle," I shout.

"Like bald eagle?" DeShon chuckles. "Bird of America?"

"Strong, powerful. It fits you, Addy. I mean, Adaugo."

I stop, turn around. (Jay's serious. He's not making fun of me.)

"It means different in Africa."

"What's it mean?"

"Hold up. Be still."

Everyone quiets.

Quick patters, rustling sounds.

"Look." A small stampede bursts from the forest. Plants tremor and shake.

"Bobcat," shouts Jay.

"Hush."

The bobcat races, disappears.

Amazed, we see fleeing rabbits, a skunk, mice, and raccoons. A deer leaps down the hill.

"Water. They smell water." (Of course. Our path is less steep. More bushes than trees. More dirt mixed with rocks. Fewer boulders.)

"We're going to make it," I shout.

Nessa does a shuffle, spin. Jay and DeShon clap backs like they've scored a point.

"Let's go."

"Want your boots?"

"You keep them, Nessa." I'm so happy, I don't care about sore feet.

"We're going to be okay," DeShon chortles, hopping ahead rapidly. "Keep moving."

Faster and faster. The haze is less thick. Me and Jay have adjusted to fake shoes.

Keep moving.

I smell water, too. Better yet, I can see it. The map is in my mind.

"What's Adaugo mean? In Africa?"

I smile. Jay never lets go.

"It means 'Of the air. Farseeing. Watchful.' "

Stepping, still shuffling, I think of my mind's maps. Aerial perspective.

Leo said, "You're excellent at spatial reasoning."

Who knew? Adaugo. Perfect for wilderness me.

"I'm never going to call you Addy again!"

Agreeing with Nessa, Jay and DeShon chant:

"Adaugo, Adaugo, Adaugo."

Nessa adds her bell-like pitch.

My heart beats in time. "I don't mind Addy. Less formal. Friends call me Addy." (Not true. I don't have any Bronx friends.)

"Okay!" crows Nessa.

"Ad-dee, Ad-dee, Ad-dee."

My smile slips.

Chanting, hopping, high-fiving, Nessa, Jay, and DeShon are more cheerful, alive.

(Not me.)

I'm speechless. I let my guard down.

See. I see.

Sparks light the ground, the rocky cliff like pretty twinkling Christmas lights.

I focused on the burning trees, but the undergrowth—moss, weeds, wildflowers—burns, too.

The ground cover, once cool, moist, and living, is hot, dry, and being destroyed.

"Ad-dee, Ad-dee, Ad-dee."

Ground fire is a wriggling snake, making erratic shapes.

Behind Nessa, fire rushes downward from above, toward our ledge.

I turn, look ahead. Flames light the rocky hillside on our right, making the ledge even narrower.

"Move," I scream. "Hurry." I hand Jay the flashlight. "The cliff's burning."

DeShon's still like stone.

"Behind you. Look."

Jay sweeps the beam behind us, then in front of us. "We're going to be trapped. Embers behind and ahead are burning up the trail."

"We've got to outpace it," DeShon says, his voice low, steady.

"Single file. Jay, Nessa—"

"No, Addy, I need to be next to you."

"Okay. Jay, DeShon, Nessa. Then me.

"Go around me, Nessa."

Unsteady, she inches past me. I worry.

"Let's go," hollers Jay.

On our right, the mountainside is heating up, bubbling with small pockets of fire.

Nessa holds her right arm and shoulder, trying to keep them safe.

All of us are stepping left of center, inches closer to dropping off the narrow ledge. Despite fear, we're doing okay—trying to balance, to be as good as Nessa. But in training, we weren't sleep-deprived, unable to see clearly, and choking on smoke.

I envision the Eagle's Ridge map. We're maybe thirty feet above the stream. Survivable? Maybe. Chance of being seriously hurt? High, most definitely.

"Hurry, we've got to hurry." But we can't run. The terrain is too dangerous.

Sunrays are losing the battle with smoke.

Both behind us and in front of us, ground fire spreads. Around the edges, me and Jay's book-shoes are charring.

Jay and DeShon are taking long, giant steps. Nessa's are smaller, two steps to their one.

"Too hot," she screams, swaying left.

She's going to fall.

I grab her arm, pull her body against mine. The weight slams me against the rock. I cry out. DeShon and Jay stop, turn around.

"No, go!

"DeShon, help Nessa."

We're almost there. We're almost there. My shoulder to my elbow is seared. The pain is dreadful.

Pop, pop, pop. Trees high above, smaller trees, lodged cliffside, explode. Bushes crackle and sizzle. Behind and in front, ground cover has embers, pockets of red-orange everywhere.

I smell paper burning. *Focus, Addy.* Twelve feet, maybe eleven to go.

"Run!" From this height, falling won't kill anyone.

"Just run!"

Jay bursts off full steam. DeShon's pulling, almost dragging Nessa. Without completely stopping, he lifts her off her feet and runs.

Run, Addy.

(I didn't run before. I know I didn't.)

I'm crying, frustrated, angry because I let us get trapped. Dumb, dumb, dumb. We shouldn't have rested.

(I knew better.)

Breathing hard, I harness my energy. Dash. Hurry. One last dash. No, another one. One more.

Focus.

Survive.

I dive off the trail, landing on a mixture of pebbles, sand, and dirt. I make it.

Breathing heavily, Jay and DeShon lie flat-back on the bank. Nessa's curled into a ball.

Studying the furious, burning cliff, I can't help thinking it's alive, trying to outwit us. A master maze-maker.

There's no longer a trail. Fire has erased it.

I turn onto my back. Smoke has weight—its layers press down on me. My lungs ache. I need to cough, but if I do, it'll hurt more.

My arm? I can't move my arm. I shift my head. The top half of my sleeve is burned away. My skin is red, crinkled, angry. Peeling.

During the last dash, I didn't feel anything other than my struggle to escape, breathe.

Now wave after wave of pain catches me.

I can't see stars. Yet, through layers of smoke, ash, I see the great wildfire. It's a multilevel monster overtaking Eagle's Ridge.

Caught you. I shiver.

Caught you.

Fire.

What I was most afraid of in my dreams is now real.

I cry. What difference do my maps and mazes make?

III

"Addy, you're hurt." Jay helps me sit up.

"Addy, Addy."

"Addy." DeShon and Nessa aren't happy-chanting, but still, I like them calling my name.

"I'm sorry," says Nessa. "It was my fault."

"No, it wasn't. I'll be okay."

DeShon holds the flashlight while Jay scrambles through the MedKit. Frowning, intent, he wets gauze.

"This is going to hurt."

"You're going to be a doctor," I say.

"Hold my hand," offers Nessa.

"Let her grip mine." Without giving me a

chance to decide, DeShon clasps my right hand. He nods at Jay.

I suck in air, eyes tearing, trying to swallow the pain.

"Cool a burn, cool a burn," he keeps repeating as the damp gauze feels like a match held to my skin.

DeShon's locked me in place. I'm angry that he's fit, strong now. Six weeks ago, I could've pushed him away. Escaped.

"It's done."

"The pain is worse, Jay."

He gives me two ibuprofen. Nessa hands me her water bottle.

"Last step, Addy. This cream helps with healing and pain."

I grit my teeth, clutch DeShon's hand. (I'm going to break it.)

Gently, Jay's fingertips smooth the cream into my burn. As he bandages my wound, I feel the medicines starting to work. The electrifying pain dims.

"Where'd you learn so much, Jay?" Nessa asks.

"After my younger brother was hurt"—he pauses—"I took first aid at the Y." He studies me, knowing I won't tell about his brother being dead.

"You should rest, Addy. We all should."

"Not long. We'll rest by the water. Okay?" I look at my friends.

"Okay," Jay answers, helping me stand.

Weary, we collapse. Only a few more feet, but it feels like running a mile.

(If fire doesn't kill us, exhaustion will.)

Fire rages above us and down Eagle's Ridge's side. Flare-ups die along the shoreline. Damp ground has slowed the spread. The stream swallows falling logs, branches.

"We're safe for now," I say, sliding the water canister from my backpack. "Mine's half full. Yours, Jay?"

"About half, too."

"Let's share. Two sips each."

"There's a whole stream, Addy," complains DeShon. "We can drink what we want."

"Leo taught me streams look pure but aren't always safe."

"Bacteria," warns Jay.

"Some adventure," DeShon gripes. "No water. Not even during a wildfire."

"How do you think it started?" asks Nessa.

"Probably a campfire." Jay sighs. "Someone who didn't respect the wilderness."

My eyes water, not just from the smoke. Will Paradise Ranch burn? What about Leo? Ryder and the other animals? Does Leo have an escape route?

Jay repeats Nessa's question. "Kelvin and A'Leia? Jamie, Dylan? Do you think they made it?"

"I hope so." (In the direction they were heading, I didn't see a way out of the maze. Worse, I'm superstitious. A'Leia didn't have Monty's jacket. It must've burned in the tent.)

"Here," I say. "Two protein bars. We'll split one. Save the other for later."

"I've got coconut granola."

DeShon grimaces. "Keep it, Jay. Never had granola till here. And I hate coconut."

We laugh.

"I'm going to wash my hands and face," says Nessa.

I look at Jay.

"Keep your mouth and eyes closed. You don't want an infection, Nessa," he says. "DeShon, let's see your ankle."

"You sound like a doc with that 'let's see' stuff."

"Best doc you've got, DeShon." Grinning but serious, Jay checks DeShon's swelling, his range of motion.

Trying to ignore my wound, I flip through laminated first aid cards:

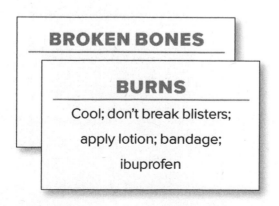

BROKEN BONES

BURNS

Cool; don't break blisters;

apply lotion; bandage;

ibuprofen

(Jay aced it!)

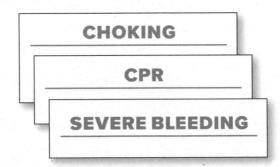

CHOKING

CPR

SEVERE BLEEDING

(I'm freaking. So much can go wrong.)

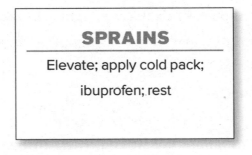

SPRAINS

Elevate; apply cold pack;

ibuprofen; rest

(I'm grateful DeShon's injury isn't worse.)

STROKE

DeShon swallows two caplets. Jay sets his back-pack underneath DeShon's foot.

DeShon can't rest. None of us can.

Swollen ankle or not, he'll have to walk on.

An engine chugs, whirls above.

"A copter. Must be a helicopter," shouts Jay. He and Nessa yell, wave their arms. DeShon, hopping on one good foot, bellows, "Here! We're here!"

I can't see the sky. No sun, no clouds. Only a veil of smoke, floating embers and ashes, pressing down. Dirty air is trapped in the valley.

Never-ending night haunts the forest.

No pilot can see us, I think. Rescue isn't going to come from a plane. They can't see us. At least, not yet.

Jay, DeShon, Nessa, screaming themselves hoarse, jump up and down, waving.

Rescue won't be easy.

I study the surroundings.

Where next?

Locked in a deep valley, I feel sorry that Leo and I didn't explore this terrain.

I close my eyes, wishing I were an eagle.

We could stay and wait to be found. Hope the fire doesn't reach the stream. But if fire doesn't stop (and it won't for days, weeks, maybe months?), the haze won't disappear. Worse, creating its own complicated path, fire could keep hopscotching over land until it overwhelms us.

We could follow the stream to the river. But for how long? How many miles? How many days would it take?

On the computer, I saw the extended map, where the stream becomes a river, bypassing a town. Maybe twenty miles. But I didn't experience it firsthand. I didn't see the landscape myself. "There's always surprises," Leo said. "A Google map doesn't show everything."

DeShon's still screaming at the sky. Jay and Nessa have given up.

"We'll rest tonight. Strike out tomorrow."

"Strike out where?"

"If we follow the stream, it'll lead us to town."

"How do you know?"

"I've seen it." But how to explain I don't know everything? "Leo will find us. He won't give up. And he's got Ryder. Ryder's the best explorer of all."

All three stare, skeptical.

"We don't even know that man," DeShon complains bitterly. "Leo. Leo who? We're his summer project. Black city kids—'Let's show them what they can't do,'" he mocks, furious, hopping on his good foot. "I'd be safer at home. Safer than on some stupid camping trip."

(I never expected to bring anyone else on my journey, just me. Focused.

If I were a bird, I'd leave them all.)

"You wanted to stay, DeShon," Jay says softly. "All of us did. We all learned to like it here."

Silence, except for the cracking, snapping fire above us.

DeShon collapses onto a rock, rubbing his sprained ankle. "My bad. Didn't know I liked snakes. Reptiles. Lizards are like snakes' cousins."

He grins, sheepish. "Wish I could see a crocodile. Turtles. Big ones." His hands spread wide.

"Didn't know global warming hurts reptiles. People, too. Never knew hotter weather was a problem."

"Lots of things we didn't know," mutters Jay.

"But Jamie and Dylan are our guides. They're supposed to know everything." Nessa studies the ground like it's gold. "Maybe we should've gone with them?"

More silence.

"I didn't ask you to follow me. Any of you. I just felt, believed"—I swallow—"hiking north, trying to cross in front of an oncoming fire, was wrong."

Nessa clasps her palms. "You don't think the others made it?"

"I don't know."

* * *

All I know is: To survive, you don't wait to be found.

"Addy," murmurs Jay, scooting close to me and Nessa. "We're glad we followed you." He turns and looks back at DeShon.

"True dat," answers DeShon. Then, crazily, he winks at me.

SURVIVE

I

Streams become rivers. Sometimes snow melts, smaller bodies of water merge and become strong, flowing river water. Topography teaches all water flows downhill. Gradually or suddenly.

But if it's steep, there could be rapids.

We walk. It's horrible. The stream bank is mud, muck, loose sand, and pebbles. Paper shoes fall apart.

Jay encourages: "We got to do it. Just do it."

DeShon sings "Girl on Fire." His voice is a beautiful bass. Nessa claps.

I don't sing. I'm paying attention. Ignoring the pain in my arm as best I can.

*   *   *

Not seeing daylight, it's impossible to know how many hours we've been awake.

The stream is getting wider and wider. We must be closer to the river.

We hike on. Dirty, mud oozing.

I keep track of the fire. It's shadowing us. Moving both downward and ahead on the ridge's layered ledges. We can't shake it.

It's going to outpace us.

DeShon limps. We've got to move on. *Keep moving.*

Another hour. Or is it two? Three?

At least the mud isn't as hard on our feet.

"Stop."

Nessa squats on the muddy ground.

Jay's chest heaves. DeShon hands him a water bottle.

"We've done good. But if we stay on this side of the river, we're not going to outrun it."

"What?" Nessa's jaw drops.

DeShon complains, "You serious? I can't swim."

"I panic trying to tread water," adds Nessa.

"There's city pools in Brooklyn. But I've never been," Jay says wearily. "My dad says suburban schools have swim teams. Some even have their own pools."

"Really?" ask Nessa, eyes wide.

"Lots of Black city kids can't swim," grumps DeShon.

They all look at me.

"Breaststroke. Some." I shrug. "Not crazy about water in my face." (Or nose, eyes, mouth.)

"This is messed up," complains DeShon. "Remind me—'Don't accept white people's charity.'"

He grimaces, sits, rubbing his sore ankle. He takes off the right boot. Blood from blisters soaks his socks. (No wonder his ankle is twisted; despite the boot, his foot couldn't bear his full weight.)

No one says anything.

Jay squats at the riverbank and throws a rock. Ripples spiral outward. Logs, some rotted, some burnt, rush, twisting and bobbing in the water.

"Maybe it's not too deep, DeShon," I say hopefully.

But how can I tell? Could I throw a rock? Maybe with a rope on it? But no, it would just sink to the bottom and I'd know how far, but not the depth, not the topography. I'd need to fly over it, measuring straight down. I'd have to hold it in the air above the river. If I had a hot-air balloon, I could do it. Then I have it!—balloons fly; more importantly, they float.

My mind *sees* it, a different kind of map. I'm measuring elevation but not mountain ranges; instead, the ranges, height beneath water:

"I think I can measure the depth." I open the backpack and MedKit. I blow air into a blue latex glove, making a funny-looking balloon. I tie it off.

Then tie it to the rope, three feet from the end. I select a rock, slightly bigger than my hand, and tie it to the rope's end. Everyone watches me curiously.

"We need to get moving, Addy," says Jay.

I fling the rope and rock out into the water. The rock drags the balloon quickly under.

"Too deep here."

We walk a few hundred feet farther down the bank. The river seems much wider. Maybe it's not as deep? Maybe a change in topography?

Moving, stretching, my burnt arm aches awful. But I can't throw with my right arm. (Also, doesn't seem right if I'm not the one measuring.)

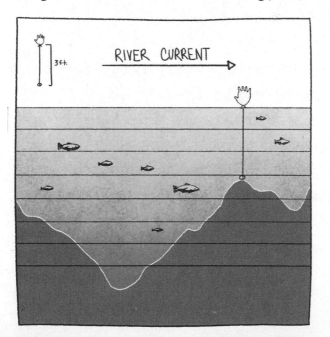

I grit my teeth. Throw.

The rope arcs, the rock splashes down. But it doesn't pull the glove beneath the water! The blue balloon bobs, almost like it's waving, in the gray current.

"What's it mean, Addy?" Nessa's voice trembles.

"Where the balloon is, it's three feet deep. We can cross here."

DeShon shakes his head.

Jay crows, "Way to go, Addy!"

(I don't say the far side of the river might be deeper.)

I look back. Fire races down the cliffside. We can't delay any longer.

"We'll try to cross here." (I don't say, *Miles back it would've been easier. Miles back when the stream wasn't a river. Miles back, I should've thought of it.*)

I start taking off my clothes. "Strip. Otherwise, clothes will weigh us down."

"Are you crazy?" asks Nessa.

"This is a horror movie," says DeShon. "This

is when we're supposed to argue. Have a knock-down, drag-out fight."

Jay chuckles. "Yeah. Say, 'Who made you boss?'"

Nessa sighs. "But when the credits roll, who survived?"

"The girl," cracks DeShon. "Usually, the girl."

We strip to our underwear, stuff our clothes in the backpacks. Tie our boots to the straps.

We all take another look at the mountainside, lit, exploding sparks, and burning faster. Too scared to be embarrassed, we step off the riverbank.

"Cold!" yells Jay. Nessa squeals. DeShon grunts.

I shiver. Weird for the air to be so hot and the water so cold. Will the water get warmer as the fire runs down to the bank? Maybe even leaps the river? No, I panic. That can't happen. If fire follows, no escape. No one survives.

"Move!" I yell.

DeShon and Jay carry the backpacks above their heads.

Me and Nessa, arms up, wade behind them.

Mud sucks between our toes. The bottom is unsteady—at times rocky, then a sudden drop-off, then soft and mossy.

Jay stumbles sideways. "Currents."

I'm shocked by their power. Water propels us downstream. We can't walk a straight line.

"It's too deep. We're gonna drown."

"Grab on to me, Nessa." As we walk farther and farther, the water rises to our chests. It's at Nessa's throat now. The rest of us are taller. But not by much.

Nessa's flailing, pulling me off-balance. Water fills my mouth and nose. Coughing, I sputter. "Not so hard. You'll drown us both."

Jay reaches for Nessa. "It's okay. It's okay. We're more than halfway. The water won't get deeper."

Nessa hears him, calms.

"You'll be okay," I say.

Jay smiles, steps backward, and slips. The backpack tilts, and he falls. We all reach for him.

Water is stronger—pushing, pushing him away, downstream. I'm screaming, "Jay, Jay!"

For now, the backpack keeps his head above water. He's kicking, trying to get to the riverbank.

"Hurry." DeShon's using all his strength to push, run through water.

Me and Nessa stay behind him. It's like he's clearing a path. Water parts around his body. "Gotta save Jay."

We step where DeShon steps—moving faster, fast as we can. We're heading toward the bank on a diagonal while brave Jay keeps kicking, as the backpack, soaked, starts to weigh him down.

He's going to drown.

Nessa's focused. No longer scared for herself.

"DeShon, get the rope," I holler. "Get the rope."

He slides onto the bank, zips open the pack, rips out the rope. I grab it, running along the bank, chasing Jay.

"Watch for the logs, Jay."

He looks at me, eyes desperate. Behind him, logs are floating straight toward him. "Catch one."

With one hand, he tries.

"Drop the backpack," I scream, racing to keep up with him. My lungs ache. My right leg cramps.

A seared log slams into him.

"Jay!" He's disappeared. "Jay." Nessa and DeShon echo me. "Jay!"

His head bursts through the surface.

He's too far. The rope won't reach. One last log spins, trapped in a swirl of current.

"Do it, Jay."

He goes under again. I keep pace, muttering, "Please, please."

He gasps as his head bobs up. His face twists with rage. He leaps, his torso up above the water, then quickly dives, catching the last log. He kicks hard, both legs splashing, churning through water.

Closer. He's getting closer to the bank.

I'm Jay's **EXIT**. His escape.

I run, faster than I've ever run before. DeShon and Nessa trail. I've got to get ahead of Jay, out-race the current.

I feel Bibi watching me. Leo, too.

*I hear: "Fly, Adaugo. Fly." Urgent, loving.
"Fly."*

I stop, cast the rope. Not far enough. I coil it back,
throw. The knotted end drops like a stone. "Kick,
Jay. Kick for your life."

See. There's one last chance. Time it right. If
I throw too soon...if I'm coiling as he floats by, I
won't get another chance. I might not get another
chance.

So, wait. Wait.

DeShon's yelling, "Throw."

Wait. Jay sees me. Mouth open, his fear match-
ing my own, he nods. Ever so slightly.

He understands.

One, two, three...I throw. The rope soars, arcs
high, then, seemingly—*slow, so slow*—drifts
down.

Jay's arm reaches high, his hand catches it. His
other hand lets go of the log. Clasping the rope
with two hands, he keeps kicking toward me.

Me, clasping tight, holding, feeling the rope

burns, my aching arm. (I won't let go.) DeShon reaches me first. He grabs the rope in front of me—puffing, pulling hard. Nessa anchors the tail.

Jay kicks; we pull. And pull.

We run to Jay, collapsed, facedown in mud. We turn him over. He's barely conscious. Worse, there's a huge gash on his side and upper thigh.

"There's an emergency blanket." DeShon grabs the MedKit from the backpack.

I tear the Mylar blanket pack open, covering Jay. DeShon grabs underneath his arms. Me and Nessa lift his feet. Together, we move Jay farther onto the riverbank. He's shivering.

I use an antiseptic wipe to clean the cut on his thigh. Jay moans but his eyes don't open.

SEVERE BLEEDING

A huge bruise wrapping from the right side to the front of his stomach. Is he bleeding inside?

I pull clothes from the backpack. Not enough.

DeShon, Nessa, and I look at each other. We all know what we have to do, but no one wants to say it. Instead, Nessa says,

"I'll collect twigs and branches."

"I'll get the heavier wood." DeShon.

I pull out the pack of emergency matches and say the horrible (necessary) words:

"We'll start a fire."

II

Jay's feverish, unconscious. Nessa and DeShon are dozing. I'm awake, worrying.

The second backpack washed up. Extra medical supplies: good. Remaining clothes—a jacket, two shirts, and pants: good, too. But wet. Rope tied between trees makes a clothesline.

From the bottom up, I study the topography—layers of water, moist soil, dry earth, rock. We're in the lowlands—no slope. Trees blaze on top of Eagle's Ridge, and pines, oaks burnt, half burnt, make crazy, pockmarked paths. I shiver. If we tried now, we couldn't climb up or hike down the ridge.

We're deep in the valley, across the river, where

the southernmost mountain mirrors the mountain to the north, across the water.

I blink, snap a picture inside my mind.

I hadn't tracked the topography on this side of the river, just the side where we escaped.

We're not safe. Only a matter of time before both sides of the mountain are on fire. One gust in the right direction could shower embers, float them across the river.

Sparklers soaring, twirling through the smoke.

Did I lead us into a dead end?

III

"Wake up. We've got to leave."

"What're you talking about?" DeShon stretches, stands. "We're safe. There'll be another helicopter. They'll find us."

"Jay can't move," cries Nessa. "We can't leave him."

I pause, studying. None of us look anything like we did when we first met. Filthy, frightened, frightful. Nessa's braids are tangled and damp, DeShon's arms muddy and scarred. Jay is limp and unconscious.

"Has the smoke lifted?" I ask wearily. We're in a strange universe. No sky, sun, or clouds.

Just smoldering air. "If there's still smoke, fire's near."

"But the fire can't cross the river," wails Nessa.

"It'll reach us. Stay here, Jay'll die. We'll all die."

Nessa buries her face in her hands.

DeShon frowns, his fingers pinching his brow.

"See any animals, Nessa? If it was truly safe, we'd see some."

"I don't want to go. I don't want to go."

"Do you see any birds? Hear an eagle? The fire will spread on this side of the river, too."

DeShon step-hops closer to me. "You had me at Jay'll die. I got an idea. Nessa, pack up, take care of Jay. Me and Addy will build a raft."

Astonished, me and Nessa stare. Then Nessa runs and hugs him. Her head barely reaches his chest; her arms squeeze his waist tight.

"What?" DeShon blushes. "I'm not stupid."

Our raft is pathetic—misshapen, odd-sized logs, braced with rope.

The surface fits two people—still-out-of-it Jay and Nessa, watchful, making sure he doesn't roll off.

Me and DeShon grip the raft tightly. He leads while I push from the back. We kick our feet, speeding us through chilling water.

I never could've imagined this: needing someone else—DeShon, no less—to find a way out of the maze.

Maybe for this moment, I dreamed? Maybe for this moment, as a kid, I survived?

No matter what happens, Jay, DeShon, and Nessa are unforgettable. Wilderness Adventures will always mean belonging to a crew, a team. Survival is more than just me.

Smoke has lessened. Slices of blue sky, white clouds appear.

"Can we stop here?" asks Nessa. "I don't smell any smoke."

"We can make camp," crows DeShon. "They'll find us."

"Miles more," I say. "Keep going. Until there's only blue sky."

Fast, splashing, I scissor my legs. DeShon does the same.

Nessa, with one hand on Jay, her other hand in the water, desperately paddles.

Never in my life have I been so tired or so cold. I almost envy Jay. Chilled, DeShon and I hold tight to the makeshift raft. Both of us pretend we're not petrified about being unable to swim.

The sky is almost clear. The wildfire seems like a monster from another life.

I hear a storm. Water falling, thunderous. I don't see rain clouds.

"Waterfall," I breathe. "Waterfall."

"What?" DeShon yells.

"A waterfall."

"You didn't say anything about a waterfall."

"There's a mist up ahead," Nessa exclaims. "The drop-off?"

"I think so. Hear it?"

Water is heavy. We hear it, slapping harsh, hissing, hitting like cement.

"Turn! Turn! To the south shore!" We could use Jay's strength, but he's still out. Nessa lays her chest on the raft, cupping water with both hands. Instead of both of us behind the raft, pushing with kicks, I move forward (hand over hand) to the raft's side. DeShon shifts, too.

We're both kicking, trying to cut the raft across the current. It isn't perfect. We're still being pushed toward the waterfall, but inch by inch, the raft floats toward the sand.

If we plunge over the falls, we won't survive.

I've never seen a waterfall, but I can hear its power.

I want to scream. I'm so mad at myself. I knew

the plunge existed. But I pushed us onward. My mind didn't remember the Google map's scale well enough. I feel guilty for insisting on a river trail I didn't know.

"We're close."

Me and DeShon turn our heads sideways. We can see where the river, foaming, falls, disappearing over a ridge.

"Kick," Nessa screams. Bravely, she slides her body between me and DeShon. Six legs kicking all together, inching toward the safe bank. An irregular, diagonal path.

"Kick," I urge. We're not just kids. We're bigger, better. Fighting for our lives, saving Jay's.

Our legs match rhythms, like paddles beating in time. Efficient, we're moving more quickly to the bank. How much time before the falls? Five minutes? Four?

Thundering, falling water gets louder.

Angry, I roar. A loud, low, guttural sound.

DeShon blasts, "Gotta make it, gotta make it."

Nessa shouts like a warrior.

Our eyes stay focused on the riverbank. Our voices battle the thrashing, booming water.

"Dig deep!" I bellow, roar.

Legs slapping water, our kicks speed up. Breathing heavy, arms pushing the wooden raft— it's not going to be enough. Another minute, we'll tumble down, down, down.

"Kick!" Adrenaline. Our hearts pound. I hear our blood rushing above the waterfall sound.

Bam.

The raft hits the bank; its bottom scrapes against sand.

Nessa's cheek slams against the raft. DeShon grabs her hand. "Stand, Nessa. We can walk."

I push up out of the water. My knees drip water on Jay's arms. "Wake up, Jay," I whisper. "Wake up." His lids stay closed.

We're safe. For how long?

Will Jay wake up?

FLYING HOME

Exhausted, we lie where we dropped.

I hear DeShon and Nessa breathing. Gradually, their lungs calm and they breathe more softly, less deeply.

I sit, watching Jay's face. Too tired to pull him off the raft, too tired to shift my position to lie beside him. Or on the riverbank.

Can you sleep sitting up? Eyes closed, head drooping on my chin, my mind flashes with pictures. Land. Sky. Fire. Water. Escaping the maze.

"Addy."

I open my eyes. Jay's awake, his gaze unfocused. I'm not sure he sees me.

"You've got to fly, Addy. Fly home."

His eyes shut before I can say a word.

Jay's not going to make it. He can't walk. He's cut, maybe bleeding inside, disoriented. My palm feels his forehead. Fever. Burning—hot fire.

"To know yourself, you need to journey, Adaugo."

I dress, restock a backpack with the rope, water. I leave the MedKit for Jay. I stuff my hoodie inside. It's dusk. Away from the wildfire, the air will cool.

"Where're you going?"

"Hey, DeShon."

"You going to leave us? Just leave us?"

Nessa stirs. "What's going on?"

DeShon's expression shifts. "Addy's leaving us," he says emphatically.

"No," Nessa sobs, hugging her knees to her chest. "A copter will find us. I know it."

"I'm going for help. Stay here—keep Jay warm. Nessa, I need my boots."

"We're safe here. Rescue will find us."

I stare at DeShon. Dirty, clothes torn, hair matted, he's been tested. We all have.

"Maybe." I stoop. "Jay's not going to last, Nessa," I say softly, carefully. "We're not trapped by the fire, but the forest still makes us hard to find. Rescuers might come, but maybe too late for Jay."

Nessa's eyes widen.

"Do what you have to do, Addy. I've got this," DeShon says, laying his hand atop Jay's motionless one. "Jay's not dying."

I blink back tears.

Nessa unties her left boot from the backpack. DeShon unties the right.

I push my feet into the boots, lacing them tight, especially around my ankles.

"At least rest," murmurs Nessa. "Leave in the morning."

I shake my head. Then tease, smiling slightly, "Don't toast any s'mores without me."

Quickly, I turn, striking out—hiking east.

II

Waterfalls are beautiful but dangerous. Just like fire.

The drop is incredible. Wish I'd known. The computer showed a decline in elevation. But nothing compares to seeing it. (It's got to be fifty feet or more.) The foam is so great, it seems like falling, frenzied snow.

Standing on jagged rocks, above the crashing water, I wish I could fly over it. Land where the water calms.

Because the incline is so steep, I have to zigzag-hike. Angle down to the left, then turn and angle down to the right. Back and forth, over and over again. (It'll take forever.)

If it weren't for pain, I'd fall asleep standing. Funny, I'm almost grateful for my burnt arm. (No one will believe burning skin smells like frying bacon.)

Still, the scars will always remind me of this escape. (If I make it.)

My supplies are low. Half-filled water bottle; a third of a protein bar. (I'm only one, compared to three: Nessa, Jay, and DeShon.)

I try not to think about them. *Is Jay alert? Is he going to die? Is Nessa crying? Searching for additional food? Are they warm enough? Will DeShon stay brave? Keep the campfire alive?*

All these questions are paralyzing. Better not to think about my friends. Just keep moving.

Move.

*   *   *

Layers of white-gray smoke make me believe I'm on an alien planet. Even with a flashlight, I can barely see in front of me. Barely avoid downed logs, boulders, and tree roots.

I feel so alone.

Fire and me. I'm locked in its maze.

The heat is too much. I'm light-headed. Smoke makes me stumble into trees; branches scratch my face and hands.

No sounds from people or animals. Only Nature: the *crackle, pop, roar* of the forest burning and the thunderous pounding of falling water.

Is the world ending?

I think about the kid we saw when we were driving to Paradise Ranch. Is he okay? His family? The horses we saw? Worry overwhelms me.

"Jamie, Dylan, Kelvin, and A'Leia," I whisper. Hoping saying their names means they're still alive. Leo, Ryder, Paradise Ranch, I can't say. (Now I'm too scared.)

What if everyone is gone?

Is it day? Night? Does it matter?

From the canister, I pour water into my eyes. Lids closed, the stinging eases.

Opening my eyes, smoke rushes back in. My eyes tear.

My chest hurts. Will I ever breathe easy again?

I want to quit. Jay said, "Fly home." I will as soon as I get back to Paradise. Get Leo to drive me to the airport.

Home. I want to go home.

I see a shadow ahead of me. *Bibi?* I stumble forward. Trickster flames. No one's there.

"There's always a way out."

I'm trying. My body is breaking down.

* * *

Wind changes direction and, like a knife cutting through smoke, I see a pathway. See a platform landing for sightseers. See wooden steps.

Pray for people.

III

Covered by waterfall mist, I step slowly. Don't want to slip. Fall. Hit my head. Break an arm.

The moisture feels good and the rushing water lifts the smoke. The steps end at a hiking trail. There's a sign: PARADISE FALLS. SCENIC VIEW.

People must come here to take photographs, to ooh and aah over the beautiful falls.

I see a small building. Bathrooms? A gift shop? I'm hopeful I can find help. Maybe a phone.

Holding the handrail, I try to move faster. Just a little bit. My legs fly out from beneath me. My butt hits hard. Off-balance, the backpack tugs me.

"Can anyone help?" I yell. No answer. Just pulsing, splashing water.

Step by step, closing in on bottom, I see a darkened cabin. A Smokey Bear sign: FIRE DANGER TODAY IS: HIGH. There's a small parking lot. Not a single car. No phone. A thick chain, like rope, blocks the entrance and exit.

I rest on the last step, frustrated and afraid. People should be here. Days ago, people were here.

I laugh, like I've never laughed before. Wild, cackling, hysterical. I stop.

I should be happy—a parking lot means a driveway means a road. A road into town.

A squeal. Then another. A staccato *kwit-kwit-kwit-kee-kee-kee-ker*.

An eagle glides, circling above me. Head tilted, I swear he sees me.

I hold my breath.

Circling, circling, circling. Daylight's gone. Shadows creep.

I can't see but I know the eagle is still there. Above me. Seeing for me.

I close my eyes.

My mind draws red arrows showing my path, escaping from the fire's maze.

My spirits lift.

EXIT—I found it.

Soar, Adaugo. Fly.

I fly higher into the blue, hovering beneath clouds.

Like the eagle, I see the whole.

Feeling renewed, I stand, ignoring my body's pain. One foot in front of the other. Hike fast. Save my friends. Save Jay.

I start running. I've finished the maze. The map is clear.

Follow the road.

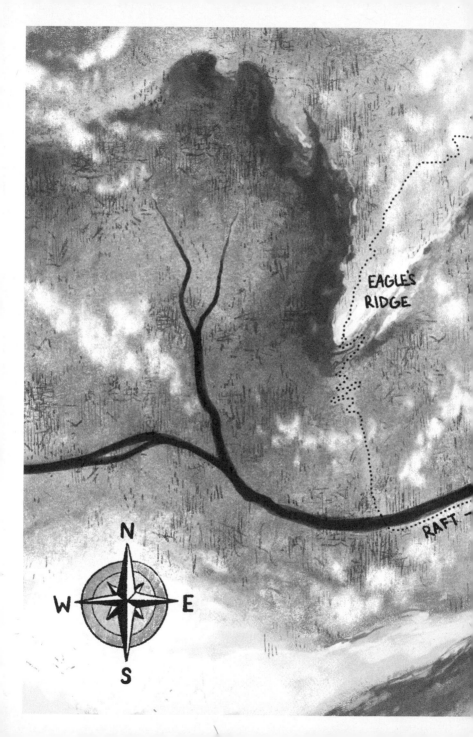

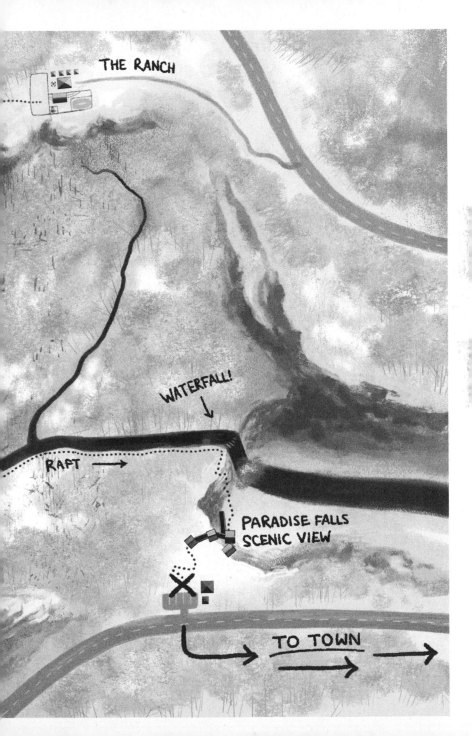

IV

Run, run, run. Breathing hard. Stitch in my side. Hiking boots, clunky on asphalt. Wish I had my tennis shoes.

Still, I run, my heel chafing inside the boot. My body aching, feeling beyond tired.

Inhale, exhale. Deep. Breathe deep.

My mind stutters: Thoughts, questions, memories jumble. Almost as if my mind is distracting me from my calf muscles tightening, slowing my pace.

Run.

The wildfire is high, above the waterfall. Smoke still rains but it's less. There's no way to tell if the fire is spreading, downward or farther east or west.

The road reflects pale moonlight. Is it nighttime or early-morning dark?

No highway lights. No cars. *Why aren't there any cars?*

Just tall oaks and pines, not burning, lining the endless road. *How long to town?*

Run.

As I tire, I walk some, run a bit, but never stop.

If I stop, I may never restart. Just unwind, fall to the ground. Fall deep asleep. *How many days has it been?*

Two. This is the third night.

I'm moving faster on the level road than I could've in the wild. Nothing to slow me down. I focus on one foot rising, the other falling, propelling me forward. Elbows up, arms loose, my heart beats rapidly. My lungs constrict; I sniff acrid smoke.

The road is narrow like a line on a map. There's nothing to see. Just trees and shadows at the edges.

Dark upon dark. But smoke is lifting. Above, patches of bright stars. A half-moon.

I'm safe. The fire is spreading elsewhere, not here.

I'm miles away from the fire. If I turn back, miles away from being able to save my friends. Only way to help is onward.

"Leo," I call. "Help me.

"Ryder," I wail.

Strange bird sounds answer me: *ca-caw* of crows, *whoop* of owls, knocking woodpeckers, and a whistling nightingale. It doesn't make sense. Day and night birds cackling, cooing, calling, singing together. Lastly, there's the eagle: *kwit-kwit-kwit-kee-kee-kee-ker.* I shiver.

My pace slows—I can't help it. Now I'm only walking. Not as good as a run, but still moving.

"Move, Addy," I say aloud. The next second I'm thinking, *Sit for a bit. Close your eyes.*

So tempting.

I drink the last sip of water.

Move.

My steps make a rocking rhythm. Lulling. Dreamy.

I'm on a daybed. A yellow blanket covering me and my cloth doll, Maya.

Hanging from the cracked ceiling are light bulbs with slow, twirling blades. Smoke spreads, spiraling outward.

"Smother it." It's Mama's voice. "Smother it."

Metal rattles. A loud bang. Mama screams.

I can't remember walking the last mile.

Shivering, gripping Maya, I sit up.

Mama swats flames in a frying pan. Pop stomps his feet. Sparks fly. Tiny flames dot the carpet. Then flames rise. Searing, suffocating.

"Mama," I mumble, still walking, sweat in my eyes.

"Adaugo," she answers.

Pop spins, falls, and writhes on the floor.

"Run, Mama," I cry out. "Move."

Mama quickly turns, striding through the smoky room.

She lifts me. Maya slips onto the floor like Pop.

"Mama," I wail, weeping, trying to rescue Maya.

Pop no longer moves.

"Fly, Adaugo," Mama whispers in my ear. "Fly."

The window is open. Mama coils inward, holding, hugging me close. Then she releases me.

I scream.

I'm flying beyond the windowsill. Flying through air.

Soaring, I see—people, streets, police cars with blinking lights, a fire truck.

I'm flying, free.

There. I see. Firefighters holding a huge trampoline-like net.

* * *

I stop crying, drop to my knees, slipping the backpack from my shoulders.

Mama saved me.
  She taught me to fly.

Headlights. Far, far off, I see high beams twinkling in the darkness.

I try to stand. But my knees buckle.

My body aches so bad. How long did I run, walk? How many hours? All night? The moon is low on the horizon.

Then the lights disappear. It must've been a mirage. A dream.

Two round wavering lights. I'm sure of it. There must've been a dip in the road.

What if the driver doesn't see me? Drives by?

I struggle to my knees. With a loud grunt, I stand.

If I stand in the middle of the road, they'll have to see me.

Beyond tired, I wave my arms above my head.

Dried mud makes my clothes darker. I hope I show up in the headlights.

The beams get close, closer. Coming fast.

I yell and yell, and then I hear the engine slow.

"Got to get Jay!" I holler. "Jay's hurt. Above the falls."

It's not Leo's van. But a red, tanklike truck. Three people get out. Firefighters in full gear. Helmets with goggles. Yellow suits with reflector strips. Heavy boots.

One of the men lifts and cradles me. A woman rushes ahead, opening the back of the emergency vehicle. Inside, I'm wrapped in a blanket, given water. Then an oxygen mask covers my entire face. My lungs expand, taking in the fresh air; my eyes blink.

The second man says, "You must be Addy."

I nod.

"Leo said if anyone would survive, it'd be you. We'll get you to a hospital."

"And Jay, Nessa, and DeShon."

"Keep your mask on. Show us instead." The woman firefighter unfolds a map.

I sigh. It's a perfect topographical map. My finger touches the paper. I trace backward from **EXIT**. Up, over the elevation lines, miles along the river (nearly halfway to Eagle's Ridge) and then I stop. My finger pokes, presses the spot. The treasure is here. My friends.

Here.

Relieved, I cry.

ESCAPE. SURVIVE.

Not one, but us.

EPILOGUE

1

Paradise Ranch. Another summer.

Leo and Jay are feeding apples to Blaze and Callie. They survived. May and Belle, too. But the piglets and chickens are new. The barn and cabins need either rebuilding or repair, but the main house made it through the fire.

Wilderness Adventures isn't open.

But there's still a new adventure. Bibi is in the kitchen. She enjoys the wild and feeding us breakfast pancakes. (We're a small team. A new family.)

The small town before Paradise Ranch is gone. People were burned; some died; some are still missing. Sometimes I see the smiling boy waving in my dreams. Is he okay?

Leo mailed me a newspaper article:

CAMPFIRE!!!!

he scrawled angrily at the bottom.

A photo showed a family, holding each other in front of a blackened mobile home. So sad. They lost everything.

Every morning, me and Ryder hike early. Leo and Jay don't join us. It's as if they know I *need* to hike alone and Ryder *needs* to hike with me.

Sometimes I think I see Jamie, Dylan, Kelvin, and A'Leia. Dylan's not being so bossy, and Jamie is happy.

Kelvin and A'Leia are holding hands. (*Best Friends Forever.*)

I worry that I could've done more to save them. All of them.

Ryder knows when I'm feeling bad. He nudges me, licks my hand.

In my jeans pocket, I carry pictures: Nessa, smiling, at a Jersey dance camp; DeShon, with headphones, cleaning reptile cages at a zoo. Thumbs up, he's looking straight out of the photo at me.

Head bowed, I sit in the porch rocker.

Still—*The journey was hard.*

Ryder plops his head on my lap. Hugging him, I rest my cheek against the soft fur on the top of his head.

Thousands of acres are scarred, dead. It's pitiful and ugly seeing remaining ash, blackened trees and ground. Some trees still stand but don't have branches that bloom leaves.

Global warming. Climate change.

I'm going to become an environmentalist. Teach and warn people to take better care of our world—for ourselves, animals, Nature, and the planet.

* * *

It's not hopeless. Me and Ryder see every day how the forest is slowly, gradually resurrecting. Regrowing.

For now, I map. Redraw the land and the wild that's been lost and what's struggling to survive.

Leo says, "It'll be decades. Maybe a hundred years before the forest flourishes again."

Next week, all of us are going to Eagle's Ridge to plant new trees.

The eagles are back. One, in particular, watches me. I watch him.

See the whole. Map the whole.
   Hard doesn't mean impossible.
   All of us need to help the world survive.

AFTERWORD

Paradise on Fire was initially inspired by the Camp Fire, which was ignited by a faulty transmission line on November 8, 2018. At the time, it was the most destructive fire in California and the most damaging fire in a hundred years. A total of 153,336 acres and 18,804 structures burned. Several towns, including Paradise, were nearly destroyed; seventeen people were injured; and eighty-five people (residents, two prison inmate firefighters, and three firefighters) died.

While I was revising my novel during the summer of 2020, California, Oregon, and Washington erupted with a lingering season of monumental fires. While the COVID-19 pandemic kept me inside my Seattle apartment, I experienced ten days with smoke so thick outside, I couldn't see the sky, Lake Union, or the mountainous skyline.

Worse, my home air purifiers worked overtime to dispel the pollution (especially the lung-scarring particulates).

As of September 17, 2020, California alone had experienced more than 8,200 blazes, with 4 million acres burned.

Climate change is impacting our planet in multiple, devastating ways. Three key elements of climate change are precursors to extreme wildfires: above-average temperatures, drought, and dry trees and other vegetation. Since 2011, severe California drought has killed almost 150 million trees; these trees became fuel for ferocious fires.

A startling fact, though, is that 97 percent of wildfires are ignited by people! Faulty power lines, campfires, fireworks from gender-reveal parties, and cigarettes all have wrought great physical and emotional destruction. Wildlife, like people, has lost habitats and has either been killed or wounded.

Climatologists also cite data that demonstrates how human activities such as using fossil fuels, raising livestock, and cutting down forests (particularly the rain forest) create global warming.

Paradise on Fire, I hope, will be a reminder to everyone that human action can slow climate change and help prevent forest fires. Human inaction can accelerate climate change and make it more likely that even the most accidental of ignitions will create environmental, psychological, and financial damage to our nation.

Paradise on Fire was also inspired by African American teens I met while giving a speech for the Jackson Hole Writers Conference. The audience was majority white, and after my speech, I reached out to everyone, but especially the six or so Black youth. I learned they were part of City Kids, a Washington, DC, program that mentors youth and runs a summer wilderness program in Wyoming. From my own experience, I knew that many city youth never experience national parks, never learn camping and hiking skills, and never learn to swim and enjoy water sports. This resonated with me because only when I became an adult did I realize there were wilderness areas to explore and landscapes like Washington State (my current home) that soothed my soul. My daughter became a Girl Scout, but it was my husband (who is white) who joined all the overnight hikes. He taught our children how to swim, snorkel, row, mountain bike, backpack, camp, and ride horses. My impoverished, segregated childhood *never* exposed me to such skills and pleasures. Of course, I, "Mama Bear," taught my kids many valuable things. But I watched as my daughter, in particular—like my character Addy in *Paradise on Fire*—grew increasingly inspired and comfortable in the wilderness.

According to the 2020 Surveys of National Parks, minority visitation is low: less than 2 percent African American, 5 percent Asian American, and 5 percent Hispanic American.

Just as I didn't know Black women wrote books until I was a junior in college, I believe systemic racism affects communities of color in terms of their awareness and access to wildlife and nature. Science has demonstrated that Nature is good for human happiness and health. What are the consequences, then, of millions of kids not having access to or feeling ill at ease with wilderness activities? How will such deprived youth grow and best appreciate what causes, and what is lost because of, climate change?

While I try to write multilayered novels, I must admit I have no idea where Addy's interest in mazes and maps (especially cartography and topography) came from. From the very first scene, I knew I had to research an amazing subject. Truth be told, I'm terrible at solving mazes and reading maps. So, like Addy, I had to learn new information and skills. I guess that though I long appreciated my Pacific Northwest landscape, it was learning about geography, a map's compass rose, and real and mythic mazes, as well as how to read the signs on hand- and computer-drawn maps that proved me, at heart, a Wilderness Girl.

Who knew?

ACKNOWLEDGMENTS

Sincere thanks to everyone at Little, Brown Books for Young Readers for supporting this book. A special thanks to my Arizona State University graduate assistant, Delena Humble, for providing valuable research.

Thanks, too, to my daughter, Kelly McWilliams, who inspires me with her strength, resilience, and outdoor skills.